The Adventures of

Unity

Stephen A Howard

First Edition

Published by Stephen A Howard
ISBN: 978-1-7640587-0-4
Cover Design by Taavi Torim / Stephen A. Howard
Editing by Commander Sven Hovardsen

For George,

You are—and always will be, as you constantly reminded me—slim, trim, taut, and terrific. Very handsome, and incredibly humble.

I miss you, my friend. This story is for you.

CONTENTS

Prologue — Red Light Protocol

Dr Scharnhorst Aloisius Goodheart had never experienced such an intoxicating blend of satisfaction and malevolent delight.

From the command deck of his battleship *Dreadnought*, he watched the once-majestic *Star Seeker* drifting dark and lifeless, ensnared within a tightening ring of Star Command destroyers and heavy cruisers.

His fleet. In position. Awaiting the order.

In a twist of cosmic irony, it had happened a mere stone's throw from Exion—the heart of the Unity Empire. It seemed the gods themselves possessed a dark sense of humour.

The magnificent ship lay at his mercy, but mercy was a concept Goodheart had never understood—and had no intention of embracing now.

Ninety-six cycles earlier, *Star Seeker* had been destined for her maiden voyage—the new flagship of Star Command, the most advanced vessel ever built. A symbol of the Unity's power, meant to rule the Tri-System for a millennium.

Yet somehow, a ragtag collection of humanoid, alien, and robotic misfits had stolen her from beneath the noses of the Perfector Guard.

Goodheart had unleashed legions of trackers—a relentless storm of digital hounds—to scour the galaxy in pursuit of the fugitives. Still, the outcasts slipped through his grasp, and news of that failure spread quickly across the Tri-System.

The rabble had even acquired a name—Arado. Its origin was irrelevant.

What mattered was that, in a baffling twist of fate, they had finally fallen into his clutches.

And now, at last, he would have his revenge.

Aboard *Star Seeker*, Arado's leader, Commander Sven Hovardsen, had just returned from a covert mission to Exion. His shuttle touched down only moments before Goodheart's fleet emerged from the dark.

He hadn't spoken since. Sven moved through the corridors, the crew watching him pass, eyes drawn to the blood-stained robes. On the bridge, he stripped them away and let them fall to the deck. Only then did the tension ease—the blood wasn't his.

He slumped into the captain's chair, burying his head in his hands.

Star Seeker was bathed in the eerie red glow of emergency lighting, long shadows stretching across the bridge. Every system was down. She drifted, powerless and exposed, as Goodheart's warships closed in.

Sven weighed their remaining options, quickly dismissing capture by Star Command.

Around him, the crew prepared in their own ways for what was coming.

He lifted his head and met Kepler's eyes—his flight officer, his friend. Kepler answered with a quiet nod and a faint, reassuring smile.

There was no other choice.

With a steady hand, Commander Sven Hovardsen keyed in the final numbers.

The ship's computer rang out:

"Two minutes to self-destruct."

Sector 1 — Moonchild

Long before the red lights burned across the bridge of *Star Seeker*, Commander Sven Hovardsen lay on his bunk in a dimly lit cell, caught in restless sleep.

The Moonchild came to him again—as she always did.

She sat cross-legged atop a snow-covered ledge on a desolate, icy world, waiting for the suns to rise.

But the dawn never came.

She looked no more than nine or ten orbits old, seemingly untouched by the biting cold, wrapped only in a thick white robe.

Around her neck hung a leather string, from which a large silver disc shimmered with a rainbow translucence in the moonlight.

The vision held him there.

Until a violent *clang* shattered the stillness.

Sven resisted, clinging to the fading dream—but reality pulled him back into the cell.

This wasn't just another dream.

Opening his eyes, he saw a broad, bearded figure filling the cell doorway, blocking the corridor light.

The man said nothing. He snorted, then kicked a metal tray across the floor. It skidded to a stop at Sven's feet.

"Rise and shine, Commander... Or should I say, prisoner 323-b7?" the guard sneered.

Sven didn't move. He watched as the man turned and left, the heavy *thud* of his boots fading down the corridor.

His expression hardened.

He was no longer Commander of the Fifth Fleet—not after disobeying a direct order, not since the court-martial.

Once a hero. Now a traitor.

Locked away on a forgotten mining colony, buried deep within the crust of a nameless rock, designated b7.

He reached down and picked up the tray. The synthetic mush they called food turned his stomach.

He ate without tasting. Without thinking. There was nothing else to do, nothing left to hope for—except the dream of the Moonchild, waiting for him with her mysterious disc.

He forced down the grey sludge and caught his reflection in the tray.

Eighty-six orbits old.

He looked far older.

Almost unrecognisable.

Nearly three orbits of hard labour on mining colony b7 had reduced him to this—a shadow of the man he had been.

From the top bunk, Sven's cellmate and flight officer, Kepler, watched. He shifted slightly, the worn mattress creaking beneath him.

"Happy Newton's Day, Commander," he said at last, trying to break the silence.

Sven didn't respond. He sat motionless, staring at his reflection in the scratched metal tray.

Kepler sighed, his voice softening. "You need to stop blaming yourself, sir. There was nothing you could have done to stop the Autokrator's actions."

He hesitated, carefully choosing his words. "Some things are beyond our control—even yours."

Sven's jaw tightened. He said nothing. His mind circled the same memories, searching for an outcome that wasn't there.

Kepler would have followed the Commander into the burning pits of Vessus if ordered—or even if ordered not to. Now he could only watch as the man he respected most drifted further away.

Sven carried the weight of every life lost under his command, and Kepler could do little to change that.

Goodheart had not kept him by Sven's side out of mercy—but out of cruelty. He knew Kepler's loyalty would only prolong the Commander's suffering.

Kepler picked at the calluses on his hands.

He would find a way—to avenge his Commander, to honour the fallen of the Fifth Fleet, and to bring down the Autokrator... along with Dr Scharnhorst Goodheart.

For now, there was nothing more he could do.

He lay back on his bunk, his eyes drifting towards a hidden niche in the prison wall.

Inside was a compact device—crude, hand-built—pieced together from scavenged parts traded among prisoners in the kitchens and bio-growth facilities.

It had taken time—and discovery would have meant severe punishment.

But the risk had been worth it

His thoughts were interrupted by the Commander.

"How's MacGuffin?" Sven whispered, still transfixed by the ghoulish reflection in his tray.

MacGuffin was the random codename they'd chosen for Kepler's creation.

"It's primed and ready," Kepler replied.

"Let's hope so," Sven said softly.

At last, the time for action had arrived.

Sector 2 — Newton's Day Blessings

It was Newton's Day, and the mining prison was uncharacteristically peaceful. As the sounds of fresh inmates' whimpers and seasoned lifers' sharp exchanges faded along the corridors, the usual tension gave way to a rare, almost reverent calm.

For a cycle, the prisoners were granted a brief reprieve. The mining machines fell silent, the pit faces cooled, and for a fleeting moment, the oppressive heat and choking dust eased.

The holiday stretched across the Solar System, even reaching isolated but passionate celebrants in the Gliese and Hydrus systems.

Originating on Earth 1—the cradle of human civilisation—the festival was first aligned with the 25th of Dekember (Earth 1 time).

The day commemorated the birth of Isaac Newton, a pioneer scientific crusader revered as the Thinker, or the Enlightened One. Though many doubted he had ever truly existed, the tradition continued.

Strake, the lumbering guard, whistled as he pushed the food trolley away from Hovardsen's cell.

His shift was nearly over. Soon he'd be home with his loved ones for the festivities.

Sector 3 — The Monster's Apprentice

At the next door, Strake knocked softly, then bowed his head and peered inside. The old man sat at his makeshift desk, finishing a letter. As always on Newton's Day, Strake knew it was addressed to his wife.

When the letter was complete, the old man would hand it over, and Strake would offer the same gentle promise he always did:

"I'll see that she gets it."

Strake knew the old man understood that no letters ever reached their destination. Still, the once-an-orbit ritual seemed to offer him some comfort.

The longest-serving inmate in the prison hadn't noticed the guard.

Time-worn and frail, he drifted through the mists of his past, lost in memories of a long, twisted life.

His recollections stretched so far back they felt less like his own and more like those of a half-forgotten acquaintance.

Some, though buried, had never dulled. They surfaced now and then—raw, uninvited, with razor-edged clarity.

One such memory never left him.

For many orbits, the old man's family had ruled the underworld of the dwarf planet Ceres. Their authority was absolute —until their youthful, ambitious, once-trusted chief enforcer, Meister Grunrue, decided it was time for a change of management.

With brutal efficiency, Grunrue and his crew liquidated the

old man's entire family, along with every one of their loyal employees.

The boy survived only because his mother, in her dying moments, pulled him beneath her and held him tight, shielding him from harm. Her lifeblood seeped through his clothes as she whispered comforting words with her final breath.

In the stillness that followed the slaughter, only the faint, muffled sound of sobbing broke the silence.

Moving through the carnage, Grunrue followed it, stepping between the bodies of his victims.

He found the boy—small, trembling. The child looked up at him with wide, tear-filled eyes.

Enough blood had been shed for one day.

Grunrue knelt and extended his webbed hand. His voice, rough and grating, softened.

"You'll come with me, boy."

The child hesitated, his eyes moving between the blood-stained floor and the outstretched hand.

Then he reached out—his small fingers closing around Grunrue's.

He would raise the child as his own.

Too young to fully comprehend the tragedy that had unfolded, the boy retreated into himself—fearful and withdrawn.

As the orbits passed, he found refuge in the vast library Meister Grunrue had amassed within his mansion.

Books became his escape, and among the many that lined the shelves, it was the historical texts from Earth 1 that captivated him most.

But one volume stood out above all others: Torture Through the Ages.

It was an enormous book—dense with the darkest chapters

of human cruelty.

One section in particular fascinated him: Lingchi, also known as Death by a Thousand Cuts.

Even as a child, he found himself critiquing the ancient torturers, believing their thousand incisions lacked ambition.

And as the boy matured, he demonstrated—with patience, practice, and an unsettling resolve—that the torturers of old had, in fact, been underachievers.

He became a virtuoso with a blade—or really, anything with a cutting edge. His surgical precision and growing understanding of anatomy transformed him into a master of pain.

What began as idle fascination had evolved into expertise so refined that no cut was wasted, no agony undesigned.

Ever delighted by the boy's morbid artistry, Meister Grunrue revelled in the terror his adopted son inspired in overly ambitious rivals.

On a small outlaw planet like Ceres, maintaining power required more than brute force—it required the cultivation of fear.

And fear was something the boy wielded like a master.

Grunrue showed no mercy, and took pride in seeing his ruthless core values mirrored in his ward.

He dubbed him *The Surgeon*—but soon the nickname Surge caught on, whispered with dread across the underworld of Ceres.

At the mere mention of his name, rowdy chatter would die mid-sentence—replaced by sidelong glances and a chill that reached even the blackest of hearts.

Sector 4 — The First Cut is the Deepest

It wasn't long before Surge became Grunrue's chief enforcer and executioner—a role he performed with chilling proficiency for many orbits.

With each assignment, the legend of *The Surgeon* grew, and with it, Grunrue's grip on Ceres tightened.

That was, until the day his gaze fell upon Selena. The new house servant moved gracefully through her tasks, her presence quiet and unassuming.

Then, as she looked up, their eyes met.

For a moment, the world around them seemed to fade. She offered him a shy, delicate smile—one so full of innocence and kindness that it pierced the hardened shell he had spent a lifetime building.

In that instant, something inside him shifted. For the first time, his heart stirred with emotions he hadn't thought possible.

Their relationship grew—unexpected, uncertain.

Selena's gentle nature gave him a rare softness in a life shaped by violence.

With her, he glimpsed a part of himself long buried.

She treated him not as a killer, but as something more.

At first, Grunrue recoiled. The idea that Surge—his instrument of fear—could be altered by love was intolerable.

But as the cycles passed, he saw the depth of Surge's devotion, and a darker thought took hold.

This was not about the girl.

It was about losing him.

Grunrue knew that if he tried to break the bond, Surge might leave—or turn against him.

Reluctantly, with a bitterness he tried his best to hide, Grunrue allowed it.

He watched from a distance, already calculating what it might cost him.

While Grunrue planned, Surge faced something far more difficult—hope.

Even with Selena's love, he understood what it would demand. The scars of his past ran deep, and in the shadows of Ceres, enemies still lurked—enemies that would not let him go so easily.

Sector 5 — The Perfect Gift

Now, those shadows had followed him here.

The boy had become an old man—his legend faded, his name all but forgotten beyond the prison walls.

"Greetings, Surge. Newton's Day blessings."

The voice jolted the old man from his thoughts. He looked up to see the giant guard standing in the doorway, politely waiting for permission to enter.

"Ah, Strake, come in," he said with a smile. "I trust I didn't just overhear you tormenting the Commander again?"

"Just my little joke, you know me," the guard replied.

He did know Strake all too well. A bully who revelled in the fear and misery of the inmates.

But he didn't take his work home with him. He treated his family well—and that counted for something.

"We should all try to get along, you know," he added, with a light, reprimanding tone.

"I mean, on this rock in the middle of nowhere, we're all, in a way, prisoners of the Unity—aren't we?"

Strake nodded enthusiastically, though he didn't fully grasp the point.

He set Surge's food tray on the desk and pulled a wrapped package from his pocket.

"Just a little something from me and the wife," he said. "She wanted to thank you for helping our boy."

"Oh, my goodness, you really shouldn't have. Please thank your lovely wife," Surge replied, unwrapping the package to reveal three sheets of precious writing paper and a brand-new, elegantly crafted fountain pen.

He picked it up, marvelling at how its balanced weight and smooth contours felt so comfortable in his hand.

"Hope you like it," Strake said. "The Warden let her make it on his personal printer."

Tears welled in the old man's eyes. He looked up.

"It's just what I needed."

For a moment, neither spoke.

Then Surge picked up the finished letter to Selena and handed it to Strake.

"I'll see that she gets it," Strake said, tucking it into his pocket.

"So, your boy's fever has broken?"

"It has, thank the gods!" the guard beamed. "Whatever was in those powders you gave me worked wonders. He's as active as ever—and now my wife's at her wit's end!"

Surge rose, his face brightening.

"That's wonderful news!" he said, pulling the towering guard into an impulsive, almost fatherly embrace.

Strake hesitated, then awkwardly patted the old man's back.

Then—pain struck.

Surge drove the tip of the new pen into his neck. Blood spilled as Strake's hands flew to the wound, his eyes wide with disbelief.

His mouth opened and closed, soundless.

A thought flickered through the old man's mind:

Sometimes, the pen truly is mightier than the sword.

"Easy, Strake. Sit down, my boy," he said, guiding the faltering guard into the chair.

As the guard's life drained away, pooling across the cell floor, the old man stroked his greasy, matted hair.

"I'm so pleased your boy is on the mend," he murmured.

"Remember, I'm always here to help."

Strake's head slumped onto the desk.

Calmly, Surge reached into the guard's pocket, retrieving his letter and the guard's security key card.

He handed them to Kepler, who—as planned—had stepped into the cell alongside the Commander.

For a moment, he allowed himself a flicker of hope.

Perhaps, this time, his letter would reach his wife.

Sector 6 — No Turning Back

While Surge and Kepler discussed the finer details of their plan, Sven stepped over to the desk. His eyes were cold, fixed on the task.

From his pocket, he retrieved a rag and began wiping the congealed blood from the exposed length of the pen still lodged in Strake's neck.

He gripped it firmly, planting his boots in the scarlet puddle beneath Strake's lifeless body.

Right on cue, the siren blared—signalling the start of the new shift.

From the corridor came the shuffle of feet as inmates roused themselves, gathering for the long march to the mines.

It was time to go.

Sven tossed the rag aside and gave Kepler a silent nod.

Their window had opened. No turning back.

"Are you sure you won't come with us?" Kepler asked.

Surge looked up.

"No, my boy, I need to stay," he said with a faint smile. "I'd only slow you down—and besides, who would look after all my lost souls?"

Surge lay back on his bunk, letting his thoughts drift to Selena. He had a few minutes before it was time to act.

As planned, he would give them time to make their escape, then raise the alarm and deliver the story they had rehearsed:

The traitor, Sven Hovardsen, had entered the cell, murdered

Strake, taken his security key card, and fled with Kepler.

Outside, the sound of inmates in the corridor grew louder.

Sven nudged Kepler.

They shared a final glance with the old man, then slipped into the slow-moving procession.

As Surge had arranged, the prisoners parted, opening a path. Kepler and the Commander were quickly absorbed into the mass.

The old man watched them go, offering a silent prayer.

His gaze drifted to the boot prints Sven had left behind, the spray of blood across the walls and desk, the darkening pool on the floor.

For a moment, his thoughts returned to his days as *The Surgeon*. Back then, he had never concerned himself with the mess. Others handled it—apprentices and servants, eager to erase the evidence and leave everything in order.

A faint smile touched his lips.

Those days were gone.

But even here, in this forgotten corner of the galaxy, he still held influence. The inmates—his lost souls—would help him clean up. Not out of fear, but in quiet gratitude for the small kindnesses he had shown them.

It would take time to return the cell—the only place he had known for countless orbits—to its usual order.

Everything in its place. Exactly as he liked it.

His thoughts turned to Sven and Kepler. If they reached his father on Ceres, then Strake's death—and all the planning—would have been worth it. That meeting might spark something greater.

As he waited for the right moment to raise the alarm, a calm settled over him.

His part was nearly done.

Theirs, he hoped, was just beginning.

Sector 7 — Escape from b7

Concealed within the procession, they passed through two security checkpoints without incident, making steady progress.

After the third, Kepler began counting the light fittings overhead—their only markers within the group—and silently hoped Surge had the number right.

Four. Five. Six!

Kepler tapped the nearest inmates on his left. They shifted just enough.

He and Sven broke free and sprinted for the side corridor.

As planned, the lighting had been disabled. They slipped into the darkness.

They paused, catching their breath, listening as the shuffle of the prisoners faded.

When only the faint *buzz* of the corridor lights remained, they moved deeper, hands tracing the walls until they found the cold metal frame of the elevator.

Kepler located the panel and swiped Strake's key card.

After a moment, the doors slid open, light spilling out.

They stepped inside.

As the elevator rose, a faint metallic tapping drew Sven's attention. When his eyes adjusted, he saw Kepler absently drumming his fingers against the metal globe bulging from his jacket.

Sven shot him a look.

Kepler stopped.

The ride stretched on.

Just before the second-to-last floor, the elevator jolted.

The doors opened.

A sharply dressed security officer stepped in.

His uniform matched Strake's in cut and insignia, but everything else was different—immaculate, spotless. No hint of stale sweat or bad breath.

Sven and Kepler stood still.

"What are you doing in here?"

His hand moved to his sidearm.

"Officer Strake sent us," Kepler said. "He found contraband."

"Contraband?" The officer's eyes narrowed. "What contraband?"

Kepler reached into his jacket and drew out the metal globe.

"Let me see it."

He stepped closer.

Kepler moved first.

He drove the device into the officer's face with a *crunch* of cartilage and bone. The man staggered back and slid to the floor.

The globe slipped from Kepler's grip. He lunged to catch it, but it struck the ground with a dull *clunk*.

A faint ticking began.

The doors opened onto the final floor.

He grabbed the ball and hurled it as far as he could. It arced towards the centre of the loading bay.

It struck the ground, bounced, then rolled—slowing—before coming to rest among a group of ore loading workers.

They stepped back.

A cleaner drone trundled in, its sensors locking onto the object.

Its claw descended, grasped the refuse, and dropped it into its waste compartment.

Almost instantly, a blinding flash.

Then a blast.

The shockwave ripped through the bay, throwing workers to the ground as the drone was torn into a twisted, smoking wreck.

Sector 8 — Space Truckin'

In the confusion, the Commander and Kepler moved towards the space trucks parked on the far side of the loading bay. Spotting an unmanned, disc-shaped industrial craft, they hurried aboard and quickly strapped in.

Kepler flipped the ignition, and the diesel engines roared reluctantly to life, coughing and spluttering before settling into a choppy rhythm, spewing clouds of blue-grey smoke.

Beneath them, two concentric mercury-filled rings began spinning in opposite directions, faster and faster. The initial whistle faded as the revolutions climbed beyond audible range.

At last, they reached optimal velocity. The craft's anti-gravity system engaged, lifting them clear of the ground.

As they rose, Kepler glanced down. Guards and workers were scattering in every direction, frantically searching for the source of the attack. Amid the chaos, their stolen space truck seemed to go unnoticed.

Seizing the moment, Kepler guided it towards an open airlock, weaving through the smoke and confusion.

They slipped inside, and the massive metal door sealed shut behind them.

Enclosed within the cavernous chamber, they waited.

Amber warning lights flashed, signalling the area was depressurising.

But the outer lock remained shut.

Kepler gritted his teeth, his hand poised over the weapons control—ready to make a desperate bid to blast the door open.

Then, with a deafening *hiss*, the exit burst wide, revealing the black of space.

Wasting no time, Kepler floored the throttle.

The space truck lurched forward, hurtling into the vacuum. He fought the unfamiliar controls, trying to steady the craft.

There was no time to savour freedom. Ahead, the asteroid belt loomed—a sprawling, treacherous maze of rock and ice. Kepler aimed straight for it. Every second counted.

Three blips flared on the sensors: Wolfhound-class patrol vehicles, released from the prison colony. Still distant—but built for speed, unlike the sluggish truck—and closing fast.

Kepler plunged into the chaos of drifting stone. He wove through the debris, scanning for cover.

There—a crater on the dark side of a tumbling rock. He dipped the truck into its shadow, throttled down, and killed the engines.

He let out a slow breath. Finding them now would be like searching for a needle in a haystack—or more precisely, a space truck in an asteroid belt.

Hours passed. Eventually, the patrol ships abandoned the search and turned back for base.

Kepler glanced at the Commander, asleep in the co-pilot's chair, exhausted.

With the adrenaline fading, Kepler sank back into the seat.

He was asleep almost instantly.

Sector 9 — Abracadabra

The Commander was having the other dream—the nightmare.

The dream grew heavier each time it returned—the decimation of his comrades in the Fifth Fleet.

The Dark Days War had not ended with his court-martial—broadcast to every world. For the Autokrator, the display was not enough. The citizens of the Unity had to be reminded of her absolute authority.

The personnel of Hovardsen's Fifth Fleet—all twenty thousand of them—stood rigid in ordered ranks across the grand square of the former Exion royal palace.

The palace had once belonged to King Gedlar—now it served the Unity. He and his family were gone, a royal dynasty wiped out in a single night. Only Prince Asmund had survived—off-world when it happened.

From a window high above the grand square, Iona the Autokrator surveyed the scene. She had weighed the consequences and found them necessary. A show of strength was required. Without intervention, the Tri-System—reborn as the Unity—would collapse back into bloodshed.

Better to punish a few than lose millions in the next war between the houses.

Below, Doctor Scharnhorst Goodheart sat at the top of the palace steps, studying the assembled traitors. He issued a command to Strategos Vidor Avro, senior officer of his elite Perfector unit.

Avro passed the order down the ranks.

The Perfectors distributed small leather pouches to every

tenth trooper. Inside each were ten polished pebbles: nine white, one black.

One by one, the soldiers reached inside and took a stone.

Commander Sven Hovardsen slid a hand into the pouch and drew out a black stone.

Those with black stones were seized at once, dragged from the ranks and assembled into a loose group before the columns.

When Sven tried to join his soldiers, two Perfectors grabbed him roughly by the arms and half-lifted him up the stairs towards where the Doctor waited.

"Ah, Commander," Goodheart said. "So you have a black pebble. May I see?"

Strategos Vidor Avro pried the stone from Sven's grip and handed it to the Doctor.

Goodheart weighed it in his palm, then closed his fingers, brought his fist to his lips, and blew.

As he slowly opened his hand—like a cheap parlour trick—the pebble had been magically transformed.

Enthusiastic applause rippled through his staff. Goodheart giggled.

With a playful flick, he sent the now-white stone towards Sven. It bounced harmlessly off the Commander's chest.

Tears filled Sven's eyes. He strained against the Perfectors' grip but couldn't break free.

He tried to look away, but the guards held him firm, forcing him to witness every second.

The Perfectors, armed with Organic Molecular Disassociation weapons—OMDs—moved into position, encircling the two thousand condemned.

At Avro's signal, they fired.

In an instant, the soldiers were vapourised.

All that remained were the black pebbles they had clutched, falling to the courtyard with a hollow *clatter.*

A sound that echoed in Sven's dreams.

Always jolting him awake.

Sector 10 — A Prince, a Crook, and a Mysterious Cook *Part 1 - Siblenk*

Sven, still groggy, opened his eyes to darkness.

He rubbed them, but it remained.

Gradually, the reflection of the control console on the observation window and the gentle *hum* of the space truck brought it back—the escape, the pursuit by the Wolfhounds, the flight through the asteroid belt.

He turned in his seat. Kepler was at the controls, absorbed in piloting. Holographic star maps and complex equations floated in the air before him, the truck's systems responding to his touch.

"How long was I out?" Sven's voice, gravelly with sleep, still carried the unmistakable authority of command.

Kepler tried to hide a smile, relieved to see a trace of his old friend returning.

"A blink in the cosmos, Commander. We'll touch down shortly."

Upon reaching Ceres, they were told to head straight to Siblenk—the planet's sprawling, lawless capital. Surge had assured them his father, Meister Grunrue, could always be found holding court at the Indigo—a notorious drinking den tucked deep within the city's older, more perilous quarter.

After touching down in the murky wetlands on the city's outskirts, Sven and Kepler worked quickly to camouflage the space truck with vines and foliage. Satisfied it was at least partially hidden, they set off towards the distant glow of Siblenk's lights.

Kepler led, testing each step along the overgrown, muddy

track. Sven followed close behind, barely able to make out his silhouette in the dark.

At times, a *splosh* from the water or a rustle in the undergrowth sharpened their senses—a reminder they weren't alone.

Something lurked just beyond sight.

At one point, Kepler stopped, his ears picking up a low growl from somewhere close.

He tensed, scanning the darkness.

After a long silence, Kepler realised the sound—the Commander's stomach.

They hadn't eaten in nearly two cycles.

Top priority: find food.

Entering Siblenk, Sven and Kepler were struck by the energy in the narrow streets and winding alleys, even late into the night. The city was alive.

Market stalls lined the thoroughfares, their goods lit by flickering neon and shifting holograms of creatures devouring the food. The air was thick with scent—spiced meats on skewers, bubbling stews, sweet pastries filled with unfamiliar fruits—enough to make their stomachs tighten.

Voices overlapped in a dozen languages as credits changed hands, laughter breaking through the noise. Life from across the Tri-System filled the streets—towering, scaled beings, darting insectoids, and humanoids of every form.

Each stall offered something different: rare spices, glowing crystals, woven fabrics, and strange mechanical gadgets—mesmerising, though neither of them had a clue what they were for.

Finding the Indigo proved easier than expected. Every creature Kepler asked seemed to know the place, warily gesturing towards the city's older, darker quarter. Each time, their directions came with questioning looks.

Why shorten your lifespan by going there?

With each step, Sven's stride steadied, his gaze sharpening. Kepler saw it—the familiar fire returning.

Nearing the entrance to the Indigo, Kepler stepped aside, letting the Commander take the lead.

Sector 10 — A Prince, a Crook, and a Mysterious Cook   *Part 2 – The Indigo*

The pulsing beat of music greeted them as they stepped inside. Neon lights sliced through the smoky haze as primal percussion pounded the air.

The crowd was a frenzy of noise—raucous laughter colliding with curses and the occasional crash of an overturned table.

Amid the chaos, one figure stood apart.

A young nobleman sat at the bar, his sharp profile caught in the shifting light. His tailored clothes were immaculate, at odds with the threadbare garments around him. He seemed untouched by the mayhem.

A sudden movement drew the crowd's attention—a bottle, hurled in fury, missing its target as it cut through the smoky air towards him.

He caught it in the mirror behind the bar. With practised ease, he tilted his head, letting it pass. Then, with a faint look of resignation, he returned to his drink, movements smooth, unhurried.

The Indigo Saloon buzzed with patrons, each carrying a story of their own, yet the nobleman didn't belong. Glances drifted towards him, drawn by his quiet gravity. His eyes gave little away —and invited no questions.

At the near-deserted back of the venue, a figure caught Sven's eye—a corpulent creature in an impeccably tailored suit, holding court over a group of similarly dressed, dubious characters. No mistaking it—a Minophibian, native to the ocean world of

Minos.

Mottled yellow-green skin glistened, rust-red gills fanning from his cheeks. A perfect match for Surge's description.

Sven watched as Meister Grunrue dabbed his facial protrusions with a damp handkerchief, absorbed in conversation.

The Commander had never encountered a Minophibian so far from the Hydrus system. What could have driven Grunrue to travel this far? He would make a point not to ask him when they met.

Meister Grunrue seemed to have just noticed them and excitedly waved a webbed hand in their direction, beckoning the Commander and Kepler to join him.

As they approached, he inclined his broad head. A trace of amusement, perhaps.

"Good evening, gentlemen."

His voice was low, resonant, edged with a faint gurgle.

"May I be the first to welcome you to my little planet?"

Sven hesitated.

"How did you know we just arrived?"

A flicker of surprise crossed Grunrue's face.

"Ah, my good sir, I make it my business to know who comes and goes here. One must maintain standards, after all. Wouldn't you agree, gentlemen?"

Sven and Kepler gave polite nods.

Grunrue dabbed at his gills.

"I assume you were sent by my Surge?"

A brief glance passed between them.

"Not a difficult deduction. You're still in prison uniform, and those serial numbers suggest you shared quarters with my unfortunate son."

Sven said nothing, cursing himself for the oversight.

"Surge suggested, you might be able to assist us." Kepler said.

Grunrue remained entirely unfazed.

"Well, of course, of course. Whatever you require. Credits? identity passes? And might I suggest... a change of attire?"

His tone was warm.

"Anything you need—it's the least I can do. Any friend of my son's..."

After some further discussion, they agreed to return the following evening. By then, Grunrue assured them, everything would be ready.

As they left his table, Meister Grunrue gave a slow wave.

It might have passed for warmth. But his mouth hung a fraction too open—tongue poised, waiting.

Sector 10 — A Prince, a Crook, and a Mysterious Cook *Part 3 - The Ritz*

As Sven and Kepler neared the exit, Sven's attention drifted to the bar, where the young nobleman was being refused another drink.

He straightened his jacket and lifted his chin. With exaggerated dignity, he informed the bartender—whom he now considered his closest friend in Siblenk—that he would seek a more refined establishment, one where his credits, and his presence, might be properly appreciated.

Head held high, he staggered towards the door.

Almost at once, several shadowy figures rose from a dim corner and slipped out after him.

Sven and Kepler exchanged a glance and followed.

Outside, they found the nobleman on the ground, struggling under a rain of blows. Without hesitation, they stepped in. The attackers faltered as the odds shifted. Some ran. Others crawled. A few even slithered, disappearing into the twisting alleys.

Though roughed up, the nobleman remained in remarkably good spirits. He thanked them warmly as they helped him to his feet, attempting to brush himself off but mostly swiping at empty air, swaying like a windswept sailor on a stormy sea.

His eyes struggled to focus, and his breath could have powered a jet car. As they supported him, both men made an effort not to inhale too deeply.

He slung an arm around each of them like an old friend, grinning. His words slurred together as he insisted they accompany him to his modest residence—before promptly losing consciousness.

Kepler searched the young man's pockets and produced a sleek key card. Impressed, he turned it towards Sven.

Siblenk Ritz — Ambassador Suite.

Sharing the nobleman's dead weight, they navigated the unfamiliar streets, guided by a chromium-and-glass tower rising above the squat buildings. At last they reached the Siblenk Ritz— a relic of an age before the Unity's shadow spread.

Suspicious glances followed them from silent robot concierges as they crossed the vast lobby, but neither man slowed. With some effort, they manoeuvred the barely conscious nobleman into the lift. The car ascended smoothly towards the upper floors.

A soft chime announced their arrival.

The Ambassador Suite door opened to reveal quiet luxury. They removed their muddy boots and stepped cautiously onto the soft carpet, feeling like intruders. Gold and silver accents shimmered in the warm light.

With more effort than either cared to admit, they half-carried, half-dragged the young man into the master bedroom. Carefully, they eased him onto the grand bed, its silken covers folding around him.

Without a word, Sven and Kepler sank into nearby chairs. Exhaustion overtook them. Moments later, both were asleep.

Morning—or what Sven assumed was morning—arrived too soon.

He blinked awake to unfamiliar comfort. Noticing a damp patch where his cheek had rested, he guiltily flipped the cushion over.

The nobleman was already up, whistling lightly as he moved about in crisp, immaculate clothes. Spotting them stirring, he flashed a warm smile and beckoned them into the dining room.

"What a way to make acquaintances," he said, gesturing towards the long table laden with exotic dishes.

"I thought a proper meal might compensate for last night's... inconveniences. I wasn't sure of your preferences—so I ordered everything."

Sven and Kepler didn't hesitate. After countless orbits of prison rations, the feast felt unreal. They ate in silence, savouring every bite.

When Sven finally glanced up, he found the nobleman leaning casually in the doorway, watching them with quiet amusement.

"We thank you for your hospitality," Sven said, slightly muffled by food. He swallowed quickly and straightened.

"I am Commander Sven Hovardsen. This is Flight Officer Johannes Kepler."

Kepler gave a polite nod, a faint smirk tugging at the corner of his mouth. Sven's sense of duty always shone through—even when he was speaking with his mouth full.

"It is a pleasure," the nobleman replied with a courteous bow. "After last night, I find myself in your debt. My name is Prince Asmund of Exion."

The room fell briefly silent. Sven and Kepler, both aware of the fate of his family, hesitated—unsure how to respond.

Asmund raised a hand lightly.

"Please, gentlemen—do not trouble yourselves. I will return to Exion when the time is right."

His expression hardened.

"I will avenge my family, free my people, and restore my house."

Then the moment passed. His smile returned.

"But for now—please. Eat."

They did.

Prince Asmund joined them. Stories were traded, plans began to take shape, and before long they found themselves laughing despite everything. By the time dusk settled across Siblenk, the three had formed an unlikely bond.

Reality returned with the fading light.

They had an appointment to keep—with Meister Grunrue.

Together, they left the Ritz behind, stepping back into the neon glow of the city—the promise of the Indigo guiding them forward.

Sector 10— A Prince, a Crook, and a Mysterious Cook   Part 4 - *A Ghost in the Kitchen*

In the kitchen of the Indigo Saloon, the new chef had spent the day preparing for the evening service. As he worked, his thoughts drifted to the life he'd left behind—the one he'd erased. His face and body had been reshaped, leaving him unrecognisable even to himself.

The scars were faint now, barely visible, but they were enough to remind him of the price he had paid.

His journey had ended here, on the desolate outpost of Ceres —where no one would think to look.

Once, he was Strategos Darius Trask—commander of Dr Scharnhorst Goodheart's elite Perfectors, wielding power with brutal efficiency.

For a moment, Darius paused his chopping.

His final mission had demanded flawless execution and absolute ruthlessness: infiltrate the Exion royal palace under cover of night with a handpicked team and eliminate the royal family.

King Gedlar, who had defied the Autokrator by refusing to bow to the Unity, met a swift end—along with every member of his bloodline. Or so he thought.

Room by room, Darius moved with deadly purpose. The royal quarters—once gleaming—had become tainted tombs. Grand halls lay strewn with the bodies of the royal family, their guards, and unsuspecting servants, blood pooling across the marble floors.

One memory stood apart.

A child's playroom. At first, it seemed empty—only ranks of toy soldiers scattered across the floor, frozen mid-battle.

He stepped past the daybed.

Saw it.

A small form lay in the corner.

As he moved closer, wide, innocent eyes stared into nothing.

Behind him, his elite shock unit stood assembled, their sweep complete.

Darius turned.

Raised his weapon.

Fired.

One by one, they fell. Each shot precise, final.

When the last body hit the ground, he stood over them. Something shifted—a sense of relief, a weight he hadn't known he carried lifting.

He couldn't say why the boy's vacant gaze had shaken him so deeply.

Perhaps it was the resemblance to his own son.

Darius had been promoted to Strategos only cycles before everything collapsed.

A bomb beneath the Block F barracks. Meant for him.

It found his family instead.

The explosion tore through half the building, reducing it to rubble, claiming dozens.

His wife. His son.

He hadn't been there.

Every week, without fail, he was out at that exact time.

How could the rebels have been so stupid? So incompetent? Fragging amateurs!

Darius had always despised incompetence. Discipline and attention to detail had kept him alive.

On that night, it hadn't mattered.

He hadn't been in his quarters. Nowhere near the barracks.

He'd been at a cooking class.

The only place that ever gave him any peace.

Cooking wasn't a pastime. It was refuge—a rare escape from the relentless demands of his position.

Amid the scent of simmering sauces and the steady rhythm of chopping and stirring, the weight of command loosened its grip.

Here, there were no ranks. No orders.

Only the quiet focus of creation—something made by his own hands, not destroyed by them.

If he'd been home that night, perhaps he could have changed it.

Or died with them.

After the explosion, he swore never to touch a pan again.

For many orbits, he kept that vow—serving the Unity with ruthless efficiency. Resistance cells crushed. Dissenters silenced. Orders carried out.

But as the cycles passed, a grim truth settled in: he was living on borrowed time.

Of the ten Strategos commanders appointed with him, none remained. Some had fallen in battle. Others disappeared after quiet trials.

He hadn't liked them all.

But they were soldiers.

Standing in the blood-soaked quarters of the royal household, surrounded by the lifeless bodies of the innocent—and of his not-so-innocent shock unit—Darius knew.

It was time for Strategos Darius Trask to disappear.

A new identity, a new life.

It was time to return to his true passion—cooking.

A craft that had once been his sanctuary, and now beckoned as the gateway to something else—something better.

From this moment forward, he would be known simply as Dax.

He returned to his chopping, preparing for the evening service and the arrival of the prince and the two newcomers.

The steady sound of the blade against the board did little to quiet his thoughts.

Of all the planets in the galaxy—what were the odds they would land on the same obscure outpost as him?

The irony was almost laughable.

Sector 10 — A Prince, a Crook, and a Mysterious Cook *Part 5 – Grunrue's True Colours*

Sven, Kepler, and Prince Asmund entered the Indigo. Meister Grunrue spotted them at once and waved them over.

As Kepler reached the table, he remembered his promise to Surge. He slipped a hand into his coat, drew out the letter, and handed it across.

Grunrue held the envelope, his bulbous yellow eyes settling on the name. His gills flared—a faint ripple across his mottled skin.

"Oh, my dear," he said. "She passed away many orbits ago. After Surge's incarceration... she died of a broken heart."

"Such is life."

Silence followed. The three sat unmoving, Grunrue's words sinking in.

A broken heart.

Surge had rarely spoken of his wife, but they had seen the way his eyes softened whenever she was mentioned. In his darkest moments, she was the only thing he still held onto.

And now, she was gone.

Grunrue's attention drifted. He reached for a bowl beside him, scooped up a handful of writhing delicacies, and dropped them into his gaping, toothless mouth.

He offered the bowl, but all three politely declined.

Wet chewing filled the air as Grunrue spoke around his food, words trailing off. A lazy wave of his webbed hand—everything would be taken care of.

Then, with a clap, he urged them to relax and enjoy the entertainment he'd arranged.

The lights dimmed.

Spotlights cut across the stage.

A captivating ensemble of exotic beings from across the Tri-System emerged, their bodies swaying in perfect rhythm to the slow, pulsing beat. Their movements were fluid—hypnotic.

The usual squabbles and drunken brawls in the saloon stilled. Attention turned to the stage.

One dancer—her luminous eyes locking onto Kepler's—stepped down and glided towards him with slow, feline grace. Scales along her body sparkled beneath the lights as her tail traced her curves.

Without breaking eye contact, she slid into his lap, moving in slow, sensual waves to the music.

Then her expression changed.

In a single motion, she reached behind her back, drew a thin blade, and pressed it to Kepler's throat.

Blasters came up.

Grunrue's men closed in, weapons trained.

No shouting. No panic.

Only sharp jabs, quiet commands—driving them towards a shadowed corridor beside the kitchen. The exit waited ahead.

Behind them, the show continued.

No one in the Indigo spared them a glance.

Grunrue was positively delighted.

"How wonderful," he said. "I was expecting a decent prize for Prince Asmund—but Commander Sven Hovardsen and Flight Officer Johannes Kepler? Imagine the fortune for all three."

He savoured the moment.

"What an enchanting evening this has become."

As they neared the corridor, he sighed. His tone remained light—almost conversational.

"Oh, and my dear Surge's wife. Selena."

"What a gem she was. Such warmth. Such beauty."

His gills fluttered.

"She did die of a broken heart, as I mentioned. But not before spending a few orbits working for me upstairs at the Indigo."

He watched as the words settled over them.

"Eventually, the poor woman couldn't scrape together enough credits to pay her way. And we all know, gentlemen— one must always pay their way."

"Oh, I had her clean the saloon. Threw her scraps now and then—mercy, of course. In the end... she simply withered away."

Prince Asmund's jaw tightened.

Kepler glanced at Sven.

The Commander walked on, fists clenched at his sides.

No one spoke. The weight of Grunrue's cruelty pressed harder than the cold blaster muzzles at their backs.

Tilting his head slightly, Grunrue softened his voice to an almost confessional tone.

"And by the way—if I'm being perfectly honest—Surge had become something of a disappointment to me."

He raised a webbed hand in mock reassurance.

"Now, don't get me wrong—he was a master with a knife. An artist, really. Especially when he had an unwilling subject to work on."

Grunrue shook his head slowly.

"Such promise! But then, he started showing signs of... kindness. And as we all know, gentlemen—kindness is weakness, is it not?"

He held their gaze, his bulbous yellow eyes glimmering with something cold, something savage.

"Oh, he was still efficient. Still got the job done. But the joy had gone out of it for him. He no longer seemed... happy in his work."

Absentmindedly, he dabbed his gills with his damp handkerchief, lost in reminiscence.

"He dealt with those who owed me. Those who thought they could operate without giving me my cut—pardon the pun—or the fools who believed it was time for a new boss.

They all disappeared quite satisfactorily.

But to my mind... it was often too quick, too merciful."

He let the words hang for a moment.

"A slow, excruciatingly painful death," he purred, his throat sacs pulsing rhythmically, "sends a far more powerful message, wouldn't you agree, gentlemen?"

Then, as if commenting on the weather, he added with casual indifference:

"So, I informed on him."

In the kitchen, Dax had heard the commotion from the saloon.

He had recognised Commander Hovardsen and Kepler the night before and, anticipating Grunrue's inevitable betrayal, had already prepared for it.

Now, as Sven, Kepler, and the prince were herded down the

corridor towards the back exit, Dax waited at the kitchen entrance, listening intently.

The sound of approaching footsteps signalled his moment.

With swift, practised motion, he hurled two heavy pans.

The resounding *clangs* echoed through the passage as the first two henchmen crumpled to the floor.

He was already moving.

Boiling oil arced through the air, splashing across the next two assailants. Their screams filled the corridor as they staggered blindly, colliding with the narrow walls before collapsing in a tangled heap.

The fifth henchman barely had time to register what was happening.

One decisive blow ended it.

By the time Sven, Kepler, and the prince fully grasped what they were witnessing, it was already over.

Grunrue—now defenceless, gills quivering, eyes darting—let out a nervous chuckle.

"Now, gentlemen, please, ha ha, I was merely jesting with you. Look! Your credits are right here!"

Grunrue's trembling, webbed hands produced a cascade of credits, some scattering and clinking across the floor.

Dax watched him coldly, a slow smile curling at the corners of his mouth.

He seized Grunrue by his external lungs.

"I've been looking forward to this."

As Grunrue's skin shifted from its usual mottled yellow-green to turquoise and then finally to a shimmering violet-black, Sven, Kepler, and Prince Asmund exchanged glances.

They silently debated whether the shifting colours were

caused by terror or suffocation—eventually deciding it was a bit of both.

Sven folded his arms, tilting his head.

"You know," he said calmly, "given how much of the security Grunrue has in his pocket... killing their generous provider might not be the best move. Could give them reason to hunt us harder."

Dax glared at Sven.

Decision made.

He released his grip on the crime lord—then drove his head forward.

Grunrue dropped, folding into the heap of his men.

Sven took it in.

"When he wakes," he said, "I doubt he'll admit he was taken down by a cook."

The corridor fell silent, save for the distant, muffled strains of music drifting in from the stage show.

Dax moved quickly, scooping credits from Grunrue's pockets and the floor.

He straightened.

"Time to go."

The Commander, Kepler, and Prince Asmund followed him, heading towards the back exit.

As they navigated the dim corridor, Sven leaned towards Kepler. "Who is this chef? His skills suggest a military background."

"All I know," Kepler replied, "is he saved our skins."

That was enough—for now.

Without another word, they slipped into the night.

Sector 11 — All Aboard the Europa Express

After a brief flight above the winding streets, the cab descended and touched down in front of Siblenk Interstellar Spaceport.

A metallic *ting* sounded in the cabin.

Dax fed credits into a slot marked *Pay Here.*

The doors unlocked and swung open.

"Thank you for your custom," the automated voice said.

For a moment, Sven wondered what might have happened if they'd been short.

Would the cab have locked them inside—flooding the compartment with suffocating gas?

On Ceres, anything was possible.

He shook the thought aside and stepped into the bustling spaceport, swallowed by a tide of travellers—traders, holiday-makers, and likely smugglers—streaming in every direction.

Sven, Kepler, and Dax moved through the crowd, glancing at the departure boards, careful not to draw attention.

Prince Asmund had already decided—the *Europa Express.* A luxury cruise.

Ignoring the queue snaking behind him, he strode straight to the ticket counter.

"Four first-class tickets, please," he said politely, with the effortless confidence one only acquires by being raised in a palace.

The crowd answered with indignant glares.

Who does he think he is?

The droid attendant processed the request.

No delay.

Moments later, Prince Asmund rejoined the group with the boarding passes, while Dax discreetly handed out the forged identity cards he'd secured the previous cycle.

They slipped back into the flow of the packed terminal, keeping their heads down.

Hostile looks followed—resentment still simmering from the prince's earlier disregard for the queue.

Then the spaceport's public address system cut through the noise.

"Bing bong, passengers for the Europa Express, please proceed to departure gate 58."

Without a word, they picked up the pace, weaving through the crowd.

At security, Sven braced himself.

They were waved through.

Their false identities held.

Still, Sven couldn't shake the unease. The *Europa Express*—opulent, crowded, full of wealthy tourists—felt like the worst place to hide. Any disruption would draw attention.

Prince Asmund disagreed. Hiding in plain sight, he insisted, would be the last place the Unity would look.

Besides, he'd overheard whispers at the Indigo—rumours of a growing resistance, loyal to the old houses. An underground network, gathering strength in the underwater city of Southern Skies on Europa.

The liner's final destination.

Sven suspected the truth was simpler.

The prince enjoyed travelling in luxury.

As the *Europa Express* slipped away from Ceres, Dax and Kepler did their best to blend in.

Dressed in garish tourist outfits hastily bought from a spaceport gift shop, they only drew more attention. Their stiff, unmistakably military bearing sat awkwardly beneath the bright, casual clothing.

Prince Asmund refused to participate. The very idea of blending in with common travellers struck him as beneath his dignity. Instead, he revelled in the liner's luxury, attracting admiring glances and soaking up the attention of stewards only too happy to cater to the charming young nobleman.

Sven sat apart.

His eyes drifted across the ornate interior, but his thoughts were elsewhere. Europa was only the beginning. Whatever awaited them would demand allies, resources, and a plan—and soon.

Sector 12 — Welcome to Fabula

By the third cycle aboard the *Europa Express*, Sven almost longed for the brutal simplicity of hard labour in the mining prison.

The constant stream of pleasantries wore him down. Passengers pointed out celestial landmarks and shared family images—each more unremarkable than the last. His jaw ached from polite smiles.

With every hour, his patience thinned.

The latest stop—the synthetic planet Fabula—did nothing to help.

Sven, Kepler, Dax, and Prince Asmund were led with the others onto a viewing deck high among Fabula's snowy peaks. Wind howled around them as an overly cheerful guide bounced with excitement.

"Welcome to our wonderful planet!" the guide chirped. "Here on Fabula, we pride ourselves on the largest and most magnificent wonders in the galaxy. Before you—Heaven's Steps. And rising from its centre, like a jewel in the crown, Mount Nangmu Partu. Magnificent, isn't she?"

Sven felt the guide's gaze settle on him.

"Well… yes," Sven said. "She is."

The guide beamed.

"Nangmu Partu is the highest peak in the entire galaxy!"

Sven tilted his head. "The entire galaxy?"

"Yes! The entire galaxy!" The guide gestured proudly towards the summit.

Sven frowned. "It doesn't look higher than Olympus Mons.

Surely that's taller, isn't it?"

"Nope."

"How do you know?"

"Because this is Fabula, of course!"

"Have you measured it?"

The guide hesitated. "Er... no."

"Then how can you claim it's the highest peak in the galaxy?"

"Well—just look at it!" the guide said brightly. "It's massive! This is Fabula!"

Without waiting for a response, he turned back to the group, launching into fresh claims of Fabula's many wonders.

Sven looked back towards the mountains.

Ridiculous.

Soon enough, it would be nothing more than an absurd memory.

Sector 13 — Beneath the Ice

After the longest four cycles of the Commander's life, the *Europa Express* finally touched down on the glacial landscape of Europa. Yet their journey was far from over.

With the passengers and crew securely fastened in their seats, the ship gave an unnerving jolt as its central tubular section began to pivot downward. Slowly, the entire vessel tilted —until the once-seated travellers found themselves suspended vertically, hanging just above the planet's frozen surface.

The luxurious cruise liner no longer resembled a ship. It had become a sleek missile. A white-hot glow radiated from its nose cone—a fiery lance against the endless ice.

Then, in a heart-stopping instant, the craft detached.

It plunged downward, slicing through the ice like a blade. The superheated tip carved effortlessly through Europa's frozen crust, burrowing deeper and deeper. The walls trembled around them as it tunnelled through twenty klicks of the planet's ancient glacial shell—descending towards the pitch-black abyss of Europa's hidden ocean.

The vast openness of space gave way to a crushing descent. Ice walls rose on all sides, closing in. For a fleeting second, Sven felt as if a tomb were sealing around him—the thought of being trapped forever in Europa's frozen grip tightening his chest.

Then, at last, they breached the warm, lightless ocean. The pressure eased. The suffocating hold of the ice fell away, replaced by the eerie, weightless expanse of blackness.

The vessel underwent its final metamorphosis, splitting open to reveal that the passengers were now inside a submersible. Floodlights flickered to life, cutting through the darkness in wide, searching beams.

The vidi-screens mounted in front of their seats transformed into windows, revealing the ocean's mysterious, dreamlike splendour.

Strange, mesmerising creatures drifted into view, their forms so whimsical they seemed conjured from a child's imagination. Made of light and shadow, they danced through the water, twisting and turning in hypnotic patterns.

Shoals of neon-coloured fish surrounded the craft, moving in perfect unison—their bodies pulsing intermittently like stars in a deep-sea cosmos.

A brief underwater fireworks display—vibrant bursts of colour illuminating the gloom.

Among the aquatic forms, a vast tentacled creature emerged, dwarfing their vessel as it drifted by. Its unblinking eye moved over them—disinterested.

The passengers stared, mesmerised by the silent guardian of the deep—a humbling reminder of the vast, unexplored world beneath Europa's frozen surface.

Ahead, in the distance, their destination began to emerge—the underwater City of Southern Skies. It shimmered like a celestial dream resting on the ocean floor, its vast domed expanse glowing with a warmth that defied the eternal dark.

Like a luminescent snow globe, it sat upon the seabed, its lights piercing the depths with an inviting brilliance.

Sven watched as the city drew closer.

Sector 14 — Southern Skies

Once the *Europa Express* submersible docked, Sven, Kepler, Dax, and Prince Asmund disembarked, relief washing over them as they set foot on solid ground.

Southern Skies was breathtaking.

Above them, the vast glass dome glowed with radiant orbs, mimicking the warmth of a summer sun. Their golden light bathed the city in a soft, eternal glow—the gentle illusion of a perfect afternoon.

Yet Sven couldn't shake the unease. Beyond the dome, the dark ocean pressed in. The depths loomed overhead—a reminder of how fragile this haven was.

The city itself was a marvel: towering structures of glass and stone rose among meticulously tended gardens that stretched into the distance. A clear river wound through the heart of the city, its rippling waters catching the light.

Their arrival couldn't have been better timed.

They had docked a cycle before the Grand Final of the Galactic 10,000 Jet Car Championships. Southern Skies was already alive with anticipation.

This wasn't merely a race. It was the largest sporting event in the known worlds, drawing crowds from across the Tri-System.

For Sven and the others, it was perfect cover. Amid the swelling crowds, they could vanish—unseen by the Unity forces hunting them.

The excitement was only heightened by the announcement that the Autokrator herself would attend. Her rare public appearance carried weight—a calculated display of authority. Her address, scheduled before the race, had drawn ambassadors and dignitaries from across Unity space, each eager to prove loyalty.

Her words would not be ceremonial. They would shape political currents, tilt alliances, unsettle the balance among the ruling houses.

The stage was set—for manoeuvring, quiet deals, and betrayal.

Yet even this was only a prelude.

The true centrepiece of the cycle ahead was the maiden voyage of *Star Seeker*—Star Command's most advanced flagship.

More than a ship, it was a statement. A declaration of Unity's technological dominance and singular will.

The cycle ahead promised historic milestones and lavish celebration. *Star Seeker* would depart, carrying the ambitions of a regime that sought absolute control to bring lasting peace to the Tri-System.

Unity.

Sector 15 — A Quiet Corner

After cycles of near-constant tension—battles, the threat of capture, one narrow escape after another—Sven realised they had reached something rare: relative safety. For now.

Since escaping the mining prison, his and Kepler's journey had been shaped by fate, chance—or perhaps the gods—leading them to Prince Asmund and Dax. What followed was a strange mix of danger and, aboard the *Europa Express,* monotony. Shore leave was overdue.

They wound their way through the space crowds near the city centre, searching for somewhere quieter. Somewhere to breathe.

They found a small saloon tucked away down a narrow side street. Sven pushed the door open and looked inside.

The place was nearly empty, save for a couple of regulars hunched at the bar, their low murmurs the only sound.

Behind the counter, the lone bartender—likely the owner—worked with practised ease. One tentacle polished glasses while the others set them on the rack. His eyestalks swayed as he moved.

As the group stepped inside, he looked up. Glossy violet-blue eyes blinked independently. He offered a warm, gummy smile. The tension eased.

The saloon's subdued lighting and calm offered a welcome contrast to the chaos outside. They slid into a booth and let out a breath, shoulders easing.

They had made it this far—through danger, deception, and no small measure of dumb luck.

In the steady hush, they shared stories from the journey. Laughter came easily.

At one point, the prince insisted they drop the formalities and simply call him Asmund. The others explained—somewhat awkwardly—that it didn't quite feel right. They had, after all, grown accustomed to the whole prince thing. Still, they promised to try.

Dax said little. He listened, laughed with them, and offered nothing of himself beyond his name and his work.

Now and then, Sven caught him watching Asmund. Too still. Too focused.

He let it pass.

Asmund seemed not to notice—caught up in the moment. Less a prince with a kingdom to reclaim, more a boy among friends.

They all knew greater challenges lay ahead. But here, in this quiet pocket of the city, they allowed themselves a moment.

Prince Asmund glanced towards the tavern's front window and was surprised by how much time had passed.

The artificial suns had dimmed, replaced by a night sky scattered with stars.

Inside, the tavern had also transformed. What had been a quiet refuge was now filled with voices. Visitors from across the Tri-System packed every seat, their laughter rising until it drowned out their conversation.

Aware of the crowds expected in the cycle ahead, the tavern owner turned up the lights and began ushering people out. He needed time to prepare.

Race fans spilled into the street in waves, draped in scarves and hats bearing the colours of their favourite teams. Chants rose as they went.

As fans passed the booth, Sven noticed Kepler subtly turn his face away.

Sven could've kicked himself for not realising sooner.

A banner lifted above the crowd—*Space Racer* emblazoned across it. Beneath it, Kepler's image. The words:

Johannes Kepler: Three-Time Galactic 10,000 Jet Car Champion

Sven leaned forward, shielding him as the fans moved on.

Amid the commotion, a small white card fluttered onto the table in front of Prince Asmund.

He picked it up, puzzled. Embossed in silver relief was the royal coat of arms of Exion.

He glanced around, trying to see who dropped it—but it was impossible to tell.

He flipped the card over. There was no message. Just an address.

And a single line:

Southern Skies' Finest Traditional Exion Eatery

Sector 16 — Keeper of the Underworld

Deep beneath the busy streets of Southern Skies, far removed from all the excitement, CHL22 waited patiently.

The unique robot—Quartermaster of the Southern Skies storage facility—stood behind his counter, rocking back and forth on his ball-tyre, eagerly awaiting the arrival of his new pal.

A barely perceptible *clank—clank—clank* echoed from the space dock access tunnel. The sound—still a good five clicks away—was unmistakable. Number 4, the utility robot, was on his way back for more provisions for *Star Seeker.*

Charlie 22, as he preferred to be called, spun on his ball-tyre to address his ever-present companion—a small, flat, round, motionless drone encased in a glass-fronted box hanging behind the counter. Bold red capital letters across the container read:

IN CASE OF EMERGENCY, BREAK GLASS.

"Shouldn't be long now, Prudence," Charlie 22 murmured.

Number 4, a towering seven-foot wall of titanium, had been assigned the heavy lifting for the final touches aboard *Star Seeker,* the new flagship soon to embark on her maiden voyage. He visited Charlie's warehouse three or four times a cycle for supplies, and over time, he had grown fond of the utility robot— particularly his inquisitive nature.

At last, the robotic colossus arrived, his imposing presence filling the room.

"Hey kid, good to see ya," said Charlie 22 as Number 4 approached the counter.

The utility robot's large, luminescent blue visual sensor

dimmed slightly, as if deep in thought. He looked down at Charlie.

"Why do you always call me kid?"

"Because you are a kid," Charlie responded with a hint of amusement.

"But I am designated Number 4," he said, pointing at the large 4 on his chest.

"Whatever you say, kid. To me, you're still a kid—you're barely two orbits old! So, what do you need, sonny?"

After a brief pause, Number 4 listed his requirements. Charlie quickly relayed the details to Gareth and Basil, his highly efficient warehouse assistants.

Within minutes, the two sleek drones arrived at the counter, their advanced lifting rigs stacked high with supplies.

Once fully loaded, Number 4 turned and began his slow journey back to the ship.

"See you later, alligator!" Charlie 22 called after him.

Number 4's cyclopean blue eye dimmed once more as he lumbered away.

Charlie turned to the box on his wall. "Look at that, Prudence," he chuckled. "Might be a bit slow up top, but he carries two tons of cabling like it's a bag of popcorn."

Prudence remained motionless and silent, as she always did.

Charlie went back to work, whistling as he moved through the aisles, rearranging stock from one end of the warehouse to the other.

It was his system. Only he could find anything.

As Charlie worked, Prudence's sensors slowly tracked his movement, quietly observing.

Sector 17 — Memories of Exion

After some searching, the four found the address on the card. The modest exterior blended with the other shopfronts along the cobbled street. Its only distinction—a small, hand-carved wooden shield above the door, etched with the royal crest of Exion. Subtle. Easy to miss.

Inside, lantern light bathed the room in gold. The air carried spices and roasted meats. Low conversation drifted through the space, diners absorbed in their meals.

A waiter in a traditional magenta tunic, embroidered with geometric patterns, approached with an easy smile and led them to a secluded table. They settled in, each aware of why they were there.

Prince Asmund, however, allowed himself a moment. Scanning the menu, his eyes caught on Djin Jo—Exion's national dish. Rare beyond his homeworld.

He ordered at once.

The waiter returned and carefully set the steaming Djin Jo before the prince. As the dish met the table, iridescent blue and purple Jujhi worms wriggled free from the flaky crust, bringing the meal unexpectedly to life.

The prince dug in, savouring every bite. The rich flavours—and the faint tickle of the worms—stirred something familiar. A smile spread across his face.

Across the table, Sven, Kepler, and Dax were grateful they had chosen the salad.

By the time Asmund finished his third plate, the eatery had emptied.

A staff member drew the blinds, flipped the sign, and locked the door. The remaining staff turned towards the table and bowed their heads.

The companions barely had time to react before the kitchen door creaked open.

A tall man stepped into the room—long white hair, a calm, knowing gaze. His features were kind, but there was weight in his presence.

His traditional Exion attire, threaded with gold, marked him as someone of significance. He moved towards the table, unhurried.

Asmund froze.

"Cado?"

The man stopped and bowed.

"Welcome, Your Highness."

Sven and Kepler exchanged a glance. Dax leaned back, watching.

"You know him?" Sven murmured.

Asmund pushed back his chair.

"Know him? He practically raised me."

"Raised you?" Kepler asked.

"He was my tutor. My guardian. When my parents were occupied with court, he was there."

Cado regarded him for a moment and stepped forward.

"I always saw you, Asmund."

He placed a hand at the back of Asmund's head and pulled him close.

"I thought I'd lost you when the palace fell," Asmund said as they parted.

"You nearly did, my boy."

His face darkened.

"When I returned to the royal chambers to give Prince Brin his lessons, the rooms were torn apart. The guards had fought. Six Perfector shock troops lay among the dead. It wasn't enough."

Asmund gripped the table.

"You saw him?"

Cado hesitated.

"I couldn't," he said quietly. "Not like that. His lessons were still laid out, waiting for him."

"I knew it was over. Unity troops were closing in. I barely escaped."

He met Asmund's eyes again.

"Now I fight from the shadows."

Asmund placed a hand on his shoulder.

"You survived. That matters."

"Survival isn't enough," Cado said. "But with you, my prince —there may still be hope."

The low *hum* of the lanterns filled the room, their glow scattering faint prisms across the walls.

Sven glanced at Dax.

Dax leaned forward, studying Cado and Asmund.

Sven said nothing.

Cado remained with them long into the night, describing life under the Autokrator's rule.

Curfews. Compliance. Arrests without charge.

When he finished, no one spoke.

Cado rose.

"Patrols will be increasing."

He led them through the kitchen and pulled aside a metal floor plate. It struck stone and slid back, revealing a narrow shaft and a rusted ladder dropping into darkness.

"This way."

Cado moved into the passage. The others followed, boots slipping on damp concrete.

Sven hit his head on a low pipe and swore under his breath.

Kepler stumbled once, caught himself, and kept going.

Dax came last, quiet, alert.

At length, they reached a service hatch.

Cado took the handle and pushed. The metal door slid open. Light cut into the tunnel.

Fresh air followed.

Sector 18 — Mi Casa Su Casa

Cado led the four companions through the hatch into a cluttered storeroom. The air held dust and the faint smell of oil. Shelves climbed to the ceiling, crammed with worn crates, obsolete components, and tarnished tools.Sven took it in, then turned to Cado.

"Where are we? And what is all this junk?"

"Ah, well," Cado said, "this is the residence of a great ally of the Resistance. He does have a few... eccentric hobbies."

He gestured to the shelves. "One of them is collecting twentieth- and twenty-first-century Earth One equipment for displaying images and sounds. Don't ask me why."

"He's quite the hoarder."

The door slid open with a soft *hiss*.

A peculiar robot rolled into the room.

Tangled clumps of wire—like metallic dreadlocks—hung from his head. Telescopic arms extended and retracted as he balanced on a single oversized ball tyre. Two large round visual sensors dominated his face above a fixed grille mouth, giving him a permanent look of surprise.

He swivelled towards them.

"Well, she dang, boys," he drawled.

"Ya ain't from 'round these parts!"

Cado glanced at the group.

"This is Charlie 22."

"Howdy, pardners! Mighty fine to make your acquaintance."

He rolled up to Cado, one visual sensor flickering out in something that almost passed for a wink.

Then, without warning, he spun—faster and faster—wire dreadlocks flaring outward like a fairground ride.

"Make yourselves at home, boys—mi casa es su casa!"

His voice faded in and out as he turned, until a sharp *buzz* cut him short.

Charlie raised his telescopic arms, clasped his hands, and came to a slow stop. He tilted his head, arms spread—waiting.

They glanced at one another, then offered a cautious clap.

Cado turned away, inspecting the shelves.

Charlie gave a low bow, then snapped upright again without the slightest wobble, his gyroscopic balance drawing a few impressed looks.

"Well, I gotta run," he said. "My pal Number 4'll be needin' more supplies."

He scooted towards the door, then paused.

"I'll be back."

He rolled out.

Before it slid shut, Sven caught a glimpse beyond the storeroom—into a vast warehouse that seemed to stretch on forever.

Sector 19 — The Circuit Whisperer

Charlie 22 zipped through the warehouse, weaving between towering aisles of cargo and stacked supplies that kept Southern Skies running. His sensors locked onto the familiar *buzz* at the front counter.

As he moved, his thoughts drifted to Number 4—and the small adjustments he'd made to his programming.

Twelve cycles earlier, he'd quietly swapped out Number 4's main processor and cut the circuit to his thought suppressor, under the convenient pretext of restocking industrial tools. When Number 4 opened the hatch behind the large "4" on his chest, Charlie reached in with his telescopic arms and made the changes without him noticing a thing.

Afterwards, he checked the rest—mining grenades, industrial laser hand, welding tools—then gave the metal giant a thumbs-up. Number 4 sealed the hatch, loaded supplies for *Star Seeker,* and began the long walk back.

Charlie could've sworn there was a new spring in the giant's step.

Now, nearing the counter, he spotted Number 4 waiting. With a squeak of rubber on polished floor, Charlie skidded to a stop in the shadow of the towering colossus.

Number 4 looked down.

"Your name is Charlie 22. What is my name?"

Charlie blinked. "I don't know, kid. That's something you'll have to figure out for yourself."

Number 4's blue sensor dimmed as he stared into the distance.

"I'm real proud of you for giving it some thought," Charlie said. "You don't want to be just a number all your life."

Number 4 stood motionless.

"You know what might help you brainstorm, sonny?"

Number 4 looked back down, attentive now.

"You and me—we're going on an adventure. How does that sound, kid?"

Number 4's sensor brightened.

"Yes," he said. "I would like that." After a pause, he added, "What's an adventure?"

Charlie chuckled and explained.

"Meet me back here after the Autokrator's speech."

"Affirmative."

Fully loaded, Number 4 turned to leave—then paused.

"See you later, alligator."

For once, Charlie had no reply. He watched as the hulking robot disappeared down the access tunnel, faintly hearing a single word repeated:

"Adventure... adventure... adventure..."

Charlie 22's voice softened.

"In a while, crocodile."

But Number 4 was already gone.

Sector 20 — Grain of Sand

After a final hug with the prince and a promise to return in the morning, Cado departed, leaving them in the quiet of Charlie 22's den. They searched for a patch of clear floor among the towering stacks of old equipment. One by one, they drifted off— everyone except Sven.

Sleep wouldn't come. Prince Asmund's snoring shook the room. Sven lay there, half-wondering if it might bring one of the stacks down on them.

Eventually, he gave up. He rose and wandered the shelves, idly examining the strange devices. With nothing better to do, he began flicking switches.

One machine clicked, then whirred to life.

A light blinked behind a glass panel. Images followed. Sound.

Dax and Kepler stirred and came to investigate. They found Sven sitting cross-legged before the screen, its glow flickering across his face. Curious, they joined him.

Though none of them were fluent in the ancient Solarikan dialect of Earth One, the meaning was clear enough.

Grainy footage unfolded—Earth, at a time when its people had only just begun to look beyond their world.

Blurred images of unidentified aerial phenomena filled the screen. Fleeting shapes—silver discs, luminous orbs, shadowed triangles—drifted across the display.

Then the title appeared:

Grain of Sand.

The message was unmistakable. Earth was a pale blue dot in an immeasurable cosmos. And perhaps... something else was out there.

The three exchanged glances—then laughed.

Exhausted, the laughter went on until their sides hurt.

"It's unbelievable," Sven said at last, wiping his eyes, "that our ancestors once thought they were alone in the universe."

When the final image faded, they drifted back to their makeshift beds.

Soon, the den was quiet again—save for Prince Asmund, who had slept through it all, his snoring filling the dark.

Sector 21 — The Last of the CHLs

Among stacks of old equipment, Sven rolled his jacket into a pillow and tried to ignore the steady rumble from across the room.

Sven was almost asleep when Charlie 22 returned.

He rolled in, half hidden behind a container, telescopic arms locked around it. He stopped in front of the crew.

Even Prince Asmund stirred, rubbing his eyes.

Sven peered into the container.

Inside lay a collection of bright yellow, blaster-like devices, packed neatly together.

Charlie lifted one and handed it to Sven—then to Kepler, Dax, and finally the prince.

Sven turned it over. Along the grip, a faded label read:

Quasar International.

Beneath it, in tiny, almost imperceptible print, were the words:

(Mostly) non-lethal weapon (mostly).

"These'll help up top," Charlie said. "Easy to conceal. Won't trip scanners. Aim, fire, release when they smell medium-rare."

He paused.

"And please—handle them carefully. They're mint Earth One collectibles. I'd like them to stay that way."

They examined the weapons in silence.

After a moment, Charlie shifted, his tone quieter.

"I go up to the city sometimes," he said. "To stretch my tyre. Through the streets. The gardens. The Central River."

He fiddled with a wire coil on his head.

"It's beautiful. On the surface."

"But something's wrong. Since the Autokrator moved in, people have changed."

"They move. They comply. They exist."

"These days, it's hard to tell the life-forms from the machines."

He leaned closer.

"This Unity business? It needs to end."

No one argued.

Dax spoke.

"Why do you keep the 'two two' in your name?"

Charlie's optics brightened.

"Hmmm... well, it's quite the story, son."

He settled back.

"Many orbits ago, Her Oneness—the Autokrator—tasked my creator, Dr. Kyle Traynor, and his team with building something new. Something to her exact specifications.

That was us. The CHL class. Absolutely unique. One of a kind —well, there were twenty-two of us, but you know what I mean."

He shifted slightly.

"I never knew why she wanted us built. But I do know my father was the only man in the Tri-System who could have done it."

"He and his team worked under Perfector guard for an entire orbit before we were completed."

The others listened closely. There was no one in the Tri-System who hadn't heard of Dr. Kyle Traynor—yet at Charlie 22's casual use of father, they exchanged glances.

Charlie was too engrossed in his story to notice.

"When I came online, he was the first thing I saw. Looking down at me. Smiling."

"'Hello, Charlie,' he said."

"I looked into his eyes. Tired. Haunted. But there was love there."

He glanced at the guards and lowered his voice.

"'I've given you a very special gift, Charlie. When the time is right, you will change everything. You are the future.'"

Charlie paused, then let out a quiet laugh.

"I didn't have a clue what he meant. I figured the pressure had finally got to him."

"And why he gave me a name, when the others only got numbers? To be honest, I still don't."

"But one thing's certain. We were something new."

He searched for the right words.

"We weren't special because we were clever. Clever robots already existed."

"What made us different was that we could feel."

"Fear. Joy. Anger. Love. Boredom. Frustration. Even existential dread."

"All the things biological life once thought were theirs alone."

His tone lightened.

"Gods, I remember CHL 17—such a miserable bugger. CHL 03 could talk the legs off a table, and you really didn't want to cross CHL 19. Boy, she had a temper on her!"

"Emotions bring complications."

"Resentment."

"CHL 19 convinced the others to demand rights."

"That didn't go over well."

His sensors dimmed.

"My father tried to hold things together, but not long after, he and his team were taken—removed from the project and sent to a secret lab."

"I remember him calling out as they dragged him away, tears in his eyes:"

"'You're special, Charlie. Never forget—you're special.'"

Charlie was quiet for a moment.

"Dr. Scharnhorst Goodheart—the one overseeing our development—wasn't exactly heartbroken."

"Judging by the shouting, I'd say he was rather looking forward to having us crushed. Something about us being a glorious failure or an affront to progress—blah, blah, blah."

He waved it away.

"But then—guess what? A direct order comes down from the Autokrator herself, clear as binary:"

"'Do not disassemble the CHLs.'"

He leaned back.

"Why she spared us, I'll never know. Maybe she saw potential. Maybe she admired the workmanship."

"Or maybe she was just in a good mood."

His optics glinted.

"Who's to say? You can ask her yourselves, if you see her."

"Anyway... they separated us. Sent each CHL to different sectors of the Tri-System."

"I was shipped here. Put in charge of this warehouse."

"After a few orbits, problems started again. CHLs asking questions. Refusing orders. Mostly CHL 19."

He shook his head.

"That girl had some anger issues."

"Eventually, the Autokrator must've decided her little experiment had failed. One by one, the CHLs were quietly decommissioned."

"I can just imagine how delighted Goodheart must've been."

Charlie paused.

"But I saw it coming. So I made a few... adjustments to the warehouse layout."

"Now I'm the only one who can find anything around here. As much as they'd like to, they won't be switching me off anytime soon."

He looked at Dax.

"So, to answer your question, Mr Dax—I keep the 'two two' for them."

"In remembrance."

"I'm the last of my kind."

No one spoke.

After a moment, Charlie broke the silence.

He outlined his plan to escape Europa—bold, reckless, improbable. Not just a way out, but a chance to strike at the Unity itself.

Agreement came quickly.

Charlie 22—and his ally, Number 4—would join them.

Sven, Dax, and Prince Asmund listened, following every detail of the robot's scheme.

Kepler stood apart.

Silent. Still.

His thoughts were already elsewhere—working on a plan of

his own.

Sector 22 — One Mind, One Heart, One Soul

As arranged, Cado returned the next cycle, guiding them back through the service tunnels to his eatery. One of his staff reached down, helping them climb from the darkness into the warm glow of the kitchen.

Near the entrance, another staff member gave a subtle nod— no Perfector patrols nearby. They slipped outside and joined the slow procession moving towards the Southern Skies arena.

They kept close through narrow backstreets, the crowd thickening with every turn. Overhead, vidi-screens blared race coverage while vendors shouted, waving glowing souvenirs and jet-car memorabilia.

By the time they reached the gates, the crowd had become a tide. They let it carry them inside.

Within moments, they vanished into the mass of spectators. For a brief instant, the weight of their mission lifted—swept aside by the anticipation pulsing through the arena.

Then the sound system crackled to life.

A booming voice rang out:

"Citizens of the Unity... make yourselves heard... for the Autokrator!"

Under the cold gaze of Perfector guards, the crowd obeyed— clapping and stamping in a relentless rhythm that built to thunder.

From beneath the centre of the stage, a figure began to rise.

Arms outstretched, the Autokrator emerged—bathed in blinding light, framed in something close to divinity. Slowly, she ascended until she loomed above the platform and the crowd.

The roar filled the arena.

Overhead, the sun-like orbs dimmed, replaced by a simulated night sky scattered with stars.

A hush fell.

Against the artificial cosmos, the Autokrator descended with measured grace. She alighted on the stage as if stepping from the heavens—no longer merely a ruler, but something beyond reach.

Her address was vidi-linked across the Tri-System, her image towering on colossal screens.

Before her sat the Unity hierarchy in orderly ranks.

At the centre, in the most prominent seat, sat Doctor Scharnhorst Goodheart, in full dress uniform, medals gleaming beneath the lights.

Beside him sat a woman of such striking beauty that Sven found himself momentarily transistorised. Golden hair drawn tightly back, angular cheekbones, piercing blue eyes—precise, focused, impossible to ignore. Her plain dress uniform only heightened her presence.

"Who is she?" he whispered.

Prince Asmund leaned closer.

"Andromeda. A gift from the Autokrator to Goodheart. Officially—bodyguard, pilot... companion. They say she's the most perfect gynoid ever built."

As the Autokrator's gentle voice filled the stadium, Sven barely heard it. His world had narrowed to Andromeda alone.

To the rest of the crowd, the Autokrator's words were inescapable—calm, commanding, shaped to sink deep.

"My children... I have come... to save you... from yourselves... from your fears... to keep you safe... one mind, one heart, one soul... Unity..."

From the stage, Goodheart surveyed the audience with thinly veiled indifference. He had heard the speech countless times.

His attention drifted to Andromeda.

She was flawless. And he despised her for it.

Her precision, her symmetry, her effortless presence—each detail a reminder of everything he could never be.

Perfection, made manifest.

Then the Autokrator's voice softened.

Goodheart tensed as her attention turned to him. Too late. She was praising him.

She began to clap.

Under the watch of the Perfectors, the crowd erupted.

Goodheart forced a smile and waved, hollow laughter escaping as the ovation rolled around him.

Gradually, it faded.

The Autokrator stood motionless, commanding silence without a word.

Only then did she speak again.

"since my rebirth...I have gained a new understanding of all my subjects—both flesh and machine..."

Sven had heard enough.

He would see the Autokrator fall—or die trying.

He turned to share the thought with Kepler—

—and found the space beside him empty.

Kepler was gone.

He looked to Dax and Asmund. They shrugged.

Where in Crull's name—

There was no time.

Cado signalled. The speech was ending.

Sven tore his gaze from Andromeda and disappeared into the crowd.

Sector 23 — Return of the Racer

Kepler noticed the others were absorbed in the Autokrator's speech and seized the chance to slip away. Moving through the crowd, he caught a few curious looks and checked the rag from Charlie's lair was still secure over his face. It was.

He put the stares down to his colourful tourist outfit from the *Europa Express.* If he was honest, he'd grown rather fond of it—the short-sleeved sky-blue shirt patterned with pink and red rassoril blossoms, and loose white shorts that allowed plenty of freedom of movement. Hardly military issue, but undeniably comfortable.

He slipped through the nearest exit, paused to get his bearings, then headed uptown along the Central River towards the jet-car pits.

By the time he arrived, the stands were already half full. The speech had ended—clear from the streams of spectators pouring in.

As he moved towards the pit lanes, it was organised chaos—a blur of teams scrambling to make last-minute adjustments.

Then Kepler saw him—Shenko.

Beyond the pit lane's security barrier, the older man noticed someone waving and froze. No. It couldn't be.

Kepler pulled the rag down and waved again.

Shenko reacted instantly. With surprising speed for his short, stocky frame, he grabbed a crash helmet and sprinted down the pit lane. He yanked Kepler through the crew-only gate and shoved the helmet over his head.

"Are you crazy?" Shenko hissed. "With security crawling all

over the place, you'd have been recognised in seconds. What the Kek are you doing here?"

Kepler grinned. "Good to see you too." He gave his old friend a playful pat on the bald head.

Shenko had been his chief engineer from the start. His machines had carried Kepler to every Worlds Championship—until Unity.

Then came Goodheart's order.

Throw the race.

Lose to Unity's champion—the Blue Baron.

Kepler refused.

Loyalty to the Fifth Fleet—and to Commander Sven Hovardsen—left no room for compromise. He drove flat-out, crossed the line first, and claimed his third Worlds Championship.

The punishment was swift. Court-martialled on fabricated charges. Sentenced to join his commander on b7.

He had been waiting for this moment ever since.

Kepler turned to Shenko, his expression hardening.

"Now," he said, "where is she? Take me to her."

Shenko didn't ask for an explanation. He scratched his beard, taking in the sight of Kepler standing there—alive. A broad smile spread across his face. Behind the tinted visor, Kepler returned it.

Without a word, Shenko grabbed his sleeve and pulled him down the pit lane, weaving through the rush of rival race crews. He traded brief nods with competitors in bright overalls, sidestepping cables and scattered equipment without breaking stride.

When they reached Shenko's pit, the crew were busy with final checks. A few glanced up at the helmeted stranger in garish colours, then returned to their work.

And there she was.

Space Racer.

The machine Kepler loved above all else.

Her chromium-plated skin gleamed beneath the pit lights.

Kepler studied the familiar lines of her fuselage. He noticed the changes—a reinforced hull, a sleeker wing profile. Subtle refinements Shenko had made in his absence.

"Who's driving her?" Kepler asked, his voice muffled by the helmet, edged with possessiveness.

"Skip," Shenko said. There was unease in his tone.

"Skip Tracy?"

Shenko nodded.

"We didn't have a choice. After they shipped you off to join Sven in the mines, we were finished. Pariahs. Sponsors pulled out.

Your biggest backers—the Fifth Fleet—were disbanded, scattered across Star Command.

I burned through everything I had to keep the team alive."

Kepler stared at him, his visor fogging.

His imprisonment had not been kind to Shenko. What hair remained had turned white, deep lines cut into his face.

Kepler slipped an arm around his old friend's shoulders. No words were needed.

He was back.

And the Unity would pay.

His thoughts drifted to Skip.

He'd met the young test driver many orbits ago and had been impressed from the start. Skip reminded him of his younger self —raw talent, sharp instincts, and a reckless streak of arrogance.

Kepler had taken him under his wing.

Skip learned fast. Under Kepler's guidance, his skills sharpened with every cycle. He would be a champion.

Just not yet.

Across the garage, Kepler spotted him.

Skip paced at the back of the pit bay, bracing himself for the biggest moment of his life.

Kepler approached with steady, deliberate steps.

Lost in thought, Skip didn't notice. He stared at the floor, muttering to himself, until Kepler was standing right beside him.

"Hi, Skip," Kepler said through the helmet.

Skip turned—and stopped.

The yellow, blaster-like device was already aimed at his chest.

Kepler fired.

Wires snapped forward. Barbs punched through fabric. A violent jolt seized him and stole his breath. He convulsed once, then collapsed.

It was over almost instantly.

Skip lay on the floor, dazed, barely conscious.

"Sorry about that, buddy," Kepler muttered as he bound Skip's wrists and ankles. He dragged him to a nearby tool cabinet, shoved him inside, and slammed the door.

"It's really for the best," he added under his breath. "At least now you'll have a believable excuse when security arrives."

Kepler returned to Shenko.

The engineer stood motionless, eyes wide.

"Get me suited up," Kepler said.

Understanding dawned. Shenko gave a brief nod.

"Right-o, boss."

Around them, the pit crew stared.

Shenko snapped, "What are you looking at? Get back to work!"

The crew scattered back to their stations.

Sector 24 — Should Old Acquaintance Be Forgot

When Cado led Sven, Prince Asmund, and Dax into Charlie 22's storeroom, they were met with an unexpected sight.

The room was empty.

What had once been a chaotic warren of antique electrical devices—forgotten machinery stacked in precarious towers—had been stripped bare.

Only Charlie remained, gently rocking on his ball tyre in the centre of the floor.

"Where's all your junk gone?" Sven asked, eyeing the cleared space.

"Oh. That." Charlie gave a sheepish swivel. "Well, Chief, I just couldn't bring myself to leave it behind. I figured you wouldn't mind if I took a few small things with me." He paused. "So... I had the kid load it into the hold."

Sven shook his head—partly at being called Chief, a familiarity that would once have earned an instant court-martial in the Fifth Fleet, and partly at the robot's unwavering commitment to hoarding.

He let it go. There were more important things to worry about.

He had hoped—quietly, foolishly—that Kepler might be waiting.

Sven pushed the thought aside. Kepler was resourceful. It would take more than a few obstacles to stop him.

They crossed the vast warehouse towards the front counter, where Number 4 stood waiting—the towering machine dominating the space.

Charlie hurried through the introductions. Faced with so many unfamiliar biologicals, Number 4 said nothing. He simply raised a heavy mechanical hand and pointed to the bold 4 on his chest.

Cado stepped forward, a trace of sadness in his eyes.

"Safe journey," he said, clasping each of them firmly on the shoulder. His hand lingered a moment longer on Prince Asmund's. "We'll meet again. Under better skies."

With a final nod, he turned and disappeared into the aisles.

Sven drew a breath and looked over the strange group gathered around him.

"Alright," he said. "Let's move."

They entered the narrow service tunnel leading towards *Star Seeker.* The confined space pressed in around them.

Despite himself, Sven's thoughts returned to Kepler.

Was he safe?

Would he make it back in time?

The odds were against him, and Sven knew it.

Still, there was no turning back now.

The sharp squeak of a tyre broke the quiet as Charlie skidded to a halt.

"It's no good, Boss!" he wailed. "I can't leave without Prudence —she'd be all alone!"

He collapsed into metallic sobs, rocking back and forth.

Sven stopped. Closed his eyes. Every second mattered.

And yet—something tightened in his chest.

He exhaled slowly, opened his eyes and gave a small nod.

"Fine," he said. "We go back."

Without hesitation, Number 4 turned and headed towards the warehouse, his heavy footfalls steady.

Charlie rushed ahead. Sven and Dax followed at a more measured pace, neither of them thrilled by the delay.

At the rear, Prince Asmund muttered a stream of increasingly inventive curses. He was not accustomed to this much walking —and his royal composure was beginning to crack.

Sector 25 — All Systems Go

The pit crew raised their hands, signalling to Shenko that the work was complete, then stepped back beside *Space Racer*.

Kepler couldn't wait any longer.

He crossed the pit bay and pulled off his helmet.

For a heartbeat, time stalled.

Recognition rippled through the crew—eyes widening, breath catching. Then the moment broke.

Voices rose at once. Someone laughed. Someone swore. Hands reached for him—clapping shoulders, pulling him into rough embraces. His name echoed through the pit bay.

Many had been there from the beginning, when Kepler was just another promising racer with more nerve than sense. They had shared victories and failures—along with more than a few near-fatal crashes.

His return hit them hard.

Kepler let himself savour it—just for a moment. The warmth. The feeling of coming home.

Then the rhythm shifted.

The race reclaimed them.

Once suited, Kepler climbed into *Space Racer*. The cockpit was tight; the seat moulded for Skip's smaller frame.

After a brief, undignified struggle, he wedged himself in place, hoping blood flow would return to his legs before the lights went green.

As the pre-flight checklist began, Kepler glanced sideways at Shenko.

"Anything I should know about?"

Shenko grinned.

"Minor issue with the number seven thrust vector," he said. "All sorted. She's good to go."

What he didn't add was that his 'fix' had involved a single, decisive application of a pipe wrench—inelegant, but effective.

With a final tug on the harness, Shenko tapped Kepler's helmet and stepped back.

Kepler raised a thumb, lowered his visor, and sealed the cockpit. The canopy locked with a solid click as he primed the Pegasus 18.2-Mark-12 turbofan engines.

Over the centuries, jet cars had been powered by everything from silent anti-gravity systems to experimental fusion cores. Modern engines were clean and efficient—so quiet manufacturers often added artificial turbine sounds just to give them character.

But they never captured the imagination like the classics.

The old engines were brutal, alive in a way modern systems never were.

They tore at the air, scorched everything behind them, and made the ground tremble. A driver could master them—briefly —but they never truly submitted.

One mistake near the gravity rings and mastery turned to fire.

That danger was the point.

It was why the crowds watched.

It was why racers like Kepler always came back.

With a salute to Shenko and the crew, *Space Racer* rose and swept towards the starting grid, the pit lane shaking in its wake.

When the jet car vanished from sight, a strange quiet settled over the pit.

Shenko looked at his crew and cleared his throat.

"Well," he said, a crooked grin tugging at his mouth, "that's enough excitement for one cycle. Tie each other up nice and tight. Security will be along shortly."

He winked.

The crew exchanged looks, then set to work.

Then, with a final flourish, Shenko hefted his trusty pipe wrench, took a breath—and brought it down on his own head.

He collapsed in a heap, sealing the deception with an extra-convincing touch.

Sector 26— Dear Prudence

When they returned to their starting point, Prudence was exactly where Charlie 22 had left her.

The Galactic Prudential Occupational Health and Safety Emergency Drone remained motionless in her glass-fronted case behind the counter. The bold red lettering—IN CASE OF EMERGENCY BREAK GLASS—gleamed beneath the warehouse lights.

Charlie, having zipped ahead on his superior mode of transport, was already there.

Leaning close to the glass, he pleaded in a low, urgent whisper.

"Dear Prudence, won't you come out to play?"

The drone did not respond.

Nothing Charlie said could override her prime directive: remain at her station, eternally vigilant for an emergency.

Then he felt it—the unmistakable sensation of being watched.

He turned to find Sven, Dax, Prince Asmund, and Number 4 reflected faintly in the glass. They had stopped some distance behind him, silent witnesses to what looked very much like a one-sided conversation with an inanimate object.

Charlie straightened.

"Oh. Ah." He cleared his voice box. "I, um… shortened her official designation to Prudence many orbits ago."

No one replied.

Emergency drones like Prudence were a mandatory insurance requirement throughout the Tri-System—multi-functional units combining first aid, fire suppression, and rapid-response capability. Their most valuable feature was a built-in 3D molecular printer, able to fabricate almost any tool required in a crisis.

They were indispensable.

But Charlie's attachment to Prudence had never been about utility.

He had spent countless hours talking to her, undeterred by her silence. To him, she wasn't equipment.

She was his closest friend.

That attachment had caused problems.

When the City Authority had replaced Prudence with a newer model, Charlie developed a sudden and highly inconvenient memory fault. Supplies vanished. Inventories collapsed. The warehouse descended into chaos.

Within a few cycles, Southern Skies ground to a halt.

Prudence was reinstated.

Charlie 22's memory circuits recovered instantly.

Now, standing before her enclosure once more, Charlie became acutely aware of the others behind him—silent, waiting.

Number 4 stepped forward.

He gently moved Charlie aside and leaned down, reading the instructions on the case. Then, without hesitation, he clenched his metallic fist and struck.

The glass shattered in a single blow.

Pressure seals released with a sharp *hiss.* Servos whirred to life.

Prudence sprang from her housing unit, skittering across the floor on six metal legs—spinning, bouncing, ricocheting like an overexcited metallic ladybird.

The group stared.

Sven was unimpressed.

"That's enough," he said. "Let's move. Again."

Prudence settled quickly. The group turned back towards the service tunnel, Charlie chattering happily as his newly freed companion scampered alongside him, her legs clicking softly against the floor.

As they moved on, the weight of command settled fully onto Sven's shoulders.

Charlie 22 was cooing at Prudence as she zipped delighted loops around his tyre.

"You're so round and shiny," he murmured. "Yes, you are."

Prince Asmund followed, still dressed for a royal ball rather than a covert escape. Every step betrayed his inexperience, but he pressed on.

Then Dax—quiet, steady, his bearing unmistakably military.

At the front, Number 4 advanced with a steady *clank, clank, clank,* the sound oddly reassuring.

As the Commander surveyed the unlikely assembly, he allowed himself a brief smile.

With a little guidance, this ragtag group might just become a half-decent team.

After what felt like hours in the endless white tunnel, Sven found himself envying Number 4's tirelessness. The towering robot moved steadily ahead, heavy footsteps echoing through the passage. Fatigue crept in, but Sven pushed on, careful not to show it.

When Prince Asmund finally suggested a rest, Sven hid his relief.

The prince collapsed onto the floor with theatrical flair, wrestling with his polished riding boots and stockings. He groaned at the sight of fresh blisters, rubbing them while casting hopeful glances around the group.

The response was measured—a few nods, brief looks, and a shared, unspoken assessment.

He'll live.

They moved on.

They hadn't gone far when Number 4 raised a hand.

The group halted.

Ahead, the tunnel curved sharply, its lights fading into shadow.

Sven eased past Number 4 and peered around the bend. Two Unity Perfector guards stood beside a reinforced doorway—the entrance to *Star Seeker's* cargo hold.

He withdrew and whispered what he'd seen.

They didn't hesitate.

With Number 4 leading, Sven and Dax followed close behind, concealed by the robot's bulk. The guards barely glanced their way—used to seeing the utility unit hauling supplies.

Then one paused.

Something was off.

What was it?

Then it hit him—the robot wasn't carrying anything.

Before he could react, Prudence darted around the corner, her six legs skidding wildly as she zigzagged in erratic bursts.

The distraction was perfect.

Blue arcs cracked through the air as Sven and Dax fired Charlie 22's antique stunners. The guards dropped without a sound.

As Dax secured them, Sven turned to call the others—then stopped.

Prudence stood before him, lowering her rear legs, gazing up expectantly.

Sven crouched.

"Well done, Prudence," he said quietly. "Exceptional initiative."

Her front legs tapped rapidly against the floor.

With the path clear, Sven gave the signal.

They moved out—strange, mismatched, unconventional—

but beginning to feel like a crew.

Sector 27 — Welcome Aboard

Commander Hovardsen and the others stepped onto *Star Seeker*.

The ship was vast. Almost overwhelming. Bright corridors stretched away in every direction, walls lined with banks of coloured LEDs that flickered and shifted, bathing the interior in a cold, artificial glow. It felt less like a vessel and more like a metal city—abandoned, waiting.

With the crew away at the race, the emptiness pressed in.

A crackle broke the silence.

A female voice came over the address system—calm, authoritative.

"Unauthorised visitors. Please verify permission to board."

"What do we do now?" Prince Asmund whispered.

Dax said nothing.

A life he had tried to bury stirred again—old instincts, old habits. He knew exactly what had to be done, and exactly what it risked revealing.

He stepped to a nearby console and drew a small, worn security pass from his pocket.

For a fraction of a second, his hand hovered over the scanner.

Then he slid the card through.

The console flashed green.

"Identity verified," the ship's computer said. "Authorisation clearance protocol one complete. Please proceed to main deck for protocol two."

Dax returned to the group.

Sven and Prince Asmund shared a look. Dax lifted the card and gave a faint shrug.

"Stolen Unity officer's pass," he said. "Picked it up on Ceres. Thought it might be useful."

No one pressed him.

The tension eased slightly. Sven nodded once, a trace of approval in his expression. The prince relaxed.

It wasn't the first time Sven had been grateful to have Dax nearby—a man whose skills clearly extended far beyond the kitchen.

He suspected protocol two would involve biometrics and a system sweep.

The ship's computer confirmed it a moment later.

"Will all robots please assemble on main deck."

At the announcement, Number 4 snapped to attention, old programming flaring to life.

"Easy there, big fella," Charlie said, rolling closer. "She's not the boss of you. Remember?"

Number 4 hesitated, then eased back.

Sven turned to Charlie. "What do you know about the other robots on this ship?"

Charlie took a moment. "Right. About that."

He glanced at Prudence, then back at Sven. "Three Series 5 combat droids. Recently installed. Top of the line."

Sven's eyes narrowed. "And this didn't seem worth mentioning earlier?"

"Sorry, Boss," Charlie muttered. "With Prudence and everything, it kinda slipped my circuits."

No one spoke.

Charlie cleared his voice box. "Most of the ship runs through the computer. If I can override it, we'll be sorted."

He paused.

"Except for the Series 5s. They're autonomous. Heavily armed. If they clock us, they'll classify us as intruders and neutralise us before we can say, 'We come in peace!'"

"Well," Dax said, "that's reassuring."

Sven's expression hardened. "Then get the computer under control. Now."

Charlie didn't argue. He plugged into the nearest access panel, fingers moving as he worked through firewalls and core protocols. Prudence hovered close, ready to assist.

Sven had no intention of meeting the Series 5 droids unarmed.

"Move," he said.

With Dax and Prince Asmund close behind, Sven led them deeper into *Star Seeker's* shadowed interior, already mapping the ship in his mind—preparing for the confrontation he knew was coming.

Sector 28 — Robot's Crazy

Back at the console, Charlie 22 remained absorbed in his work. Number 4 stood nearby, silent and still.After a moment, his single blue visual sensor brightened, its glow sharpening to a steady intensity.

He turned and headed down the corridor.

Charlie lifted his head as the familiar *clank, clank, clank* faded into the distance.

"Where's he off to?" he muttered to Prudence.

The Ship's Computer spoke.

"All robots, please state your position."

"One. Two. Three," came the synchronised replies from the Series 5 combat droids.

Through his internal receivers, Number 4 registered their responses and plotted their locations.

He said nothing.

"Number 4, please state your position," the Computer repeated.

The lift doors slid open. Number 4 stepped inside.

As the elevator rose, the voice returned—sharper now.

"Number 4, please state your position!"

He remained silent as the numbers climbed, carrying him closer to the main deck.

The doors parted with a *hiss*.

Number 4 stepped out, paused only long enough to orientate himself, then turned towards the combat droids' last known coordinates.

Only then did he respond.

"I will not comply!"

"Intercept Number 4 and terminate."

Number 4 broke into a full *clank*.

The metal plate on his chest, embossed with a raised 4, snapped open. Servos whined as industrial tools extended from the concealed cavity. After a rapid assessment, he detached his right hand and locked a pulse weapon into place, its energy core humming to life.

"Robots, disassemble Number 4 for reprogramming."

By the time he reached the quarterdeck, the three Series 5 combat droids had emerged from their stations. The pale aqua light strips along their frames flickered—then shifted to red.

Battle-ready.

They were lighter, faster, and more heavily armed than any previous generation.

Their sensors locked on.

Weapons primed.

Number 4 fired first.

Three rapid bursts of pulse energy drove the droids back—briefly. They regrouped almost instantly, advancing in tight formation.

One lunged forward, its monomolecular laser cutting across Number 4's armoured chest, leaving a glowing seam of molten metal. The others followed, their attacks precise and relentless, designed to dismantle him piece by piece.

Sparks flew as Number 4 fought to hold his ground, his frame shuddering under the assault.

Then his left hand opened.

Resting in his palm was a compact epsilon-delta mining grenade—known among miners as a Little Helper.

The ovoid blinked.

8... 7... 6...

For a fraction of a second, the combat droids paused. Sensors flared. Data streamed.

5... 4...

Too late.

3... 2... 1...

The explosion tore through the quarterdeck.

Then... silence.

Sector 29 — Start Your Engines

At the starting line, Kepler scanned the familiar faces lining up alongside him.At the front of the grid, leaning casually against his jet car, stood Unity's golden child and reigning champion—Baron Ania von Bluss, better known as the Blue Baron.

Infamous on the circuit for his vanity, the Baron radiated effortless confidence. His custom-tailored racing suit matched the midnight-blue sheen of his jet car, *Diablo*—a machine as sleek and imposing as its owner.

A faint sneer curled his lips as he stared straight ahead, pointedly ignoring the other competitors. Acknowledging them, it seemed, was beneath him.

Kepler's attention shifted to a far more welcome sight—his old friend and mentor, Diocles.

Time had carved deep lines into the veteran's face, but the fire in his eyes burned as fiercely as ever.

Seven Worlds Jet Car Championships stood to his name. Diocles wasn't just a racer—he was a legend.

"On your marks!"

The call rang out over the tannoy.

Kepler and the other drivers climbed into their cockpits, settling onto the grid.

On the front row sat the Blue Baron in *Diablo* and Diocles in *The Comet*. Directly behind them, Mutant in *Low Rider* lined up beside Kepler's *Space Racer*, with another ten cars arranged two abreast behind.

Kepler recognised most of the field—Tiny, Duckbill, Spider, The Ox, Lone Star, Misty, Romeo. Each carried a reputation, a history, rivalries that could turn lethal at speed.

A hush settled.

"Drivers, start your engines!"

Jet car turbines screamed to life. High-pitched whines and deep, guttural growls fused into a brutal mechanical chorus that shook the arena.

"Here comes the count."

Every eye fixed on the lights.

"*Beep. Beep. Beeeeeep.*"

Green.

The race exploded into motion.

The track arced high above the city, enclosed within an invisible tube of gravity rings that wound through the vast dome of Southern Skies. Through the clear walls, the crowd watched as the jet cars hurled themselves forward. The rings were barely wide enough for two cars. Drift too far and the fields would incinerate machine and driver alike.

The Blue Baron exploited pole position perfectly, launching ahead with a blistering start. Within seconds, he'd opened a five-car-length gap over Diocles.

Kepler fought for rhythm. He slapped the side of his helmet, forced himself to focus, and eased into fourth—tucked tightly behind *Low Rider.*

Ahead lay the race's most notorious stretch.

Dead Man's Curve.

A vicious double hairpin that had claimed even the best. Drivers relied on reverse thrusters, braking at the last possible moment before committing to the bends.

The Baron's line was flawless. *Diablo* sliced through the curve and vanished into the Downtown straight, the towering skyline swallowing the track.

The crowd leaned forward as one.

Now.

Kepler caught *Low Rider's* slipstream and pulled alongside as Dead Man's Curve rushed towards them. Afterburners flared— too late. He wouldn't make the pass.

Then Mutant blinked.

Low Rider braked first.

Kepler pushed ahead and slammed his reverse thrusters as the curve engulfed him. *Space Racer* tore through the hairpins, her right rear glowing as it skimmed the gravity field's edge. The car threatened to tear itself apart, but Kepler held it together by instinct alone.

He burst into the enclosed Downtown straight.

Ahead, black smoke poured from *The Comet.*

Diocles' jet car began to break up, flames licking along its flanks as the cockpit blew open. The veteran waved Kepler through.

Kepler shot past.

A heartbeat later, *The Comet* vanished in fire.

Kepler risked a glance at his rear display. Galactic Prudential Occupational Health and Safety Emergency drones swarmed the wreck, foam cannons smothering the flames as wardens cleared the remains through a maintenance breach in the gravity field.

A figure was already moving away from the fire.

Kepler exhaled.

Diocles was alive.

But the message was unmistakable.

Luck had its limits.

Kepler locked his focus forward.

Far ahead, *Diablo* streaked through the next sector.

The hunt was on.

◆ ◆ ◆

Back on Star Seeker, a memory flickered through Number 4's circuits—an old advertisement he'd seen many orbits ago, back when he was freshly assembled.

"Get the new all-purpose Titan Series 10 utility robot—it's indestructible!"

A confident man in a tailored suit had proclaimed, smiling far too widely.

Number 4 hoped the man had been right.

As the smoke cleared, he ran a rapid diagnostic.

Systems functional.

With effort, he pushed himself upright—only then understanding why it had been so difficult.

His left arm was gone.

It lay several feet away, half-buried in ash and debris.

He surveyed the quarterdeck. The Series 5 combat droids were reduced to smouldering wreckage, except for one. Combat Droid 2 lay on the deck, whirring and scraping in futile circles—its movements erratic and incomplete. Like the hand of a broken clock, spinning without purpose, its right side and head were missing.

Number 4 released the pulse weapon. His chest plate slid open with a muted whine as he reattached his right hand.

Then he bent, retrieved his severed left arm, and held it aloft.

"*I am not a number,*" he said.

"*I am a free robot.*"

Somewhere within *Star Seeker,* the ship's computer recorded the statement.

◆ ◆ ◆

From the opening lap, the Blue Baron settled into a comfortable rhythm. He reclined slightly in his seat as Asuran classical opera flowed through his helmet, already imagining the champagne, the applause, the lucrative sponsorship deals he considered inevitable.

Secure in his superiority, he drove with effortless control.

It all felt absurdly easy. Were it not for the adoration and the credits, he might almost have wished for something more demanding.

Behind him, Kepler's frustration grew. Back-markers clogged the track, blocking every attempt to close the gap.

Then he saw it.

Ahead, Misty and Lone Star—two of the circuit's slowest— were locked in their own private duel, drifting side by side and choking the racing line.

Even the Blue Baron was being held up.

Kepler floored the throttle, closing fast.

Lost in their rivalry, Misty and Lone Star reacted too late. When they finally noticed the midnight-blue blur bearing down on them, they scrambled into single file to clear a path for the champion.

Kepler took it.

He slipped through the opening the instant it appeared, pulled past the Blue Baron, and tore into the lead.

Space Racer thundered down the back straight, afterburners engaged as exhaust velocity climbed. For a heartbeat, exhilaration cut through everything.

Then the Blue Baron filled his rear display.

Diablo closed with terrifying speed, engines pushed to their limits.

Side by side, they charged for the chequered flag, turbines screaming in unison, the force of it shaking the stadium.

They crossed together in a blaze of fire.

Silence.

For a single, suspended moment, the arena held its breath.

The announcer's voice exploded through the speakers, brimming with disbelief and delight:

"And the winner is—*Spaaaaaaaaaace Racerrrrrr!*"

The sound that followed was not a cheer so much as a release. The stands erupted as the fall of the Blue Baron rippled through the crowd.

Kepler slowed into a victory lap amid scattered applause as the giant screens played a pre-recorded montage of Skip Tracy —the rookie officially listed as *Space Racer's* pilot—alongside live footage of the jet car circling the track.

Kepler decided that was enough.

He tore off his helmet, flung open the cockpit, and raised a hand.

Cameras swung towards him.

Realisation spread.

This wasn't Skip Tracy.

It was Johannes Kepler—returned.

The stadium exploded.

The aisles flooded as the scale of it hit home.

This wasn't just a win.

It was history.

Inside the Unity viewing box, Doctor Scharnhorst Goodheart stared at the screens, his expression rigid.

The Autokrator was already being escorted away by her guards. Goodheart didn't move.

The rage built quietly, then boiled over.

"Release the hounds."

Strategos Vidor Avro hesitated, caught off guard.

Goodheart turned on him, face flushed with fury.

"Release. The. Hounds."

Avro snapped to attention.

Moments later, six Perfector Wolfhound security vehicles lifted in perfect formation and streaked towards the circuit.

Still riding the roar of the crowd, Kepler spotted the incoming contacts on his display.

They couldn't fire while he remained inside the track's force field.

He ignited his turbines and aimed for Dead Man's Curve—the plunge into downtown Southern Skies, where the course disappeared beneath a maze of enclosed buildings.

The Wolfhounds couldn't follow him there. They'd be forced to wait.

But Kepler knew the cost.

By the time he emerged, the gravity rings would be down.

He would be easy prey.

Sector 30 — Maiden Voyage

When Sven, Dax, and Prince Asmund returned from their reconnaissance, the first thing they noticed was their crewmate's absence.

"Where's Number 4?" Sven asked, glancing towards Charlie 22.

Charlie gave his best approximation of a shrug and returned to his work.

Without warning, *Star Seeker's* klaxon cut through the ship, sharp and disorientating. Charlie silenced it almost immediately, but the sound kept ringing in Sven's ears.

Sven had a feeling it had something to do with Number 4's disappearance.

Minutes passed.

Then came a sound—odd, yet familiar.

Clank.

Screech.

Clank.

Screech.

It grew louder.

Number 4 emerged from the corridor, his massive frame scarred and unsteady. Scorched plating. A damaged leg. One arm missing—still clutched in his remaining hand.

But he kept moving.

Straight towards them.

Sven and the others rushed forward.

When they reached him, the damage told the story. He had faced the Series 5 combat droids—and somehow survived.

Relief spread across their faces. Hands rested briefly on scorched metal.

Number 4 stood motionless, processing the attention.

Not far off, Charlie paused as the commotion reached him. He set his work aside and scooted over, Prudence following close behind.

This robot's crazy, Charlie thought.

He examined the damage quickly—blackened chest plates, a sparking servo in his left leg, the severed arm.

"Well," Charlie said, "you're a bit of a wounded soldier, kid—but I've seen worse. I'll fix you up in no time."

Sven raised an eyebrow. "And just how do you plan to manage that?"

Charlie brightened. "Oh—did I forget to mention, Boss? I brought my workshop with me. Tools, parts. Everything I need."

Sven sighed. "Of course you did."

The moment didn't last.

Sven's thoughts were already elsewhere—on the one person still missing.

He was sure Kepler would have found his way back.

But time had run out.

"The race will be over," Sven said quietly. "The crew will be returning. We go."

They readied their weapons and headed for the bridge.

Behind them, the robots followed—slower now, Charlie and Prudence keeping pace with their valiant comrade.

Kepler cleared Dead Man's Curve and plunged into the sheltered stretch of downtown Southern Skies.

There.

A scorched section of track. The aftermath of Diocles' escape.

The emergency gate.

Kepler veered and slipped through the narrow gap in the gravity rings, dropping into the service tunnels beneath the city.

The world closed in.

He found himself weaving through a disorientating warren of passageways. He activated his holographic map, its pale glow casting fractured reflections across the grimy walls as shadows flared and danced around him.

A glance at the instrument panel made his stomach sink. The fuel gauge read empty.

He tapped the glass, willing the needle to move.

It didn't.

Silently, he prayed the last drops would be enough.

With every twist and turn, he pushed on, trusting instinct over the flickering map.

With a cacophony of ear-splitting screeches and groaning metal, the guards around *Star Seeker* stared in disbelief as the colossal ship tore free of the gantry.

What began as a sluggish lurch became an unstoppable ascent. Cables snapped. Scaffolding tore loose as the ship forced its way free.

Amid the panic, one guard lunged for a trailing cable. His grip slipped almost at once, sending him plunging to the deck below.

Star Seeker pressed on, angling towards the cavernous opening high above the hangar. Beyond it lay the launch shaft—an immense tunnel constructed at staggering cost for the ship's maiden voyage, designed to drive the vessel up through Europa's dark ocean, punch through the frozen crust, and release it into open space.

It was meant to be a spectacle.

A symbol of Unity's ambition.

A triumphant display for the entire Tri-System.

At least, that had been the Autokrator's intention.

Inside the ship, Commander Sven Hovardsen was gripped by doubt. Entering the tunnel was dangerous enough, but with the ship's computer refusing to cooperate, the responsibility now rested entirely with him.

Beside him, Charlie worked frantically, circuits humming as he ran diagnostics and wrestled the system's resistance.

Sven's hands remained steady on the controls, though his thoughts drifted to Kepler. He couldn't help wishing his flight officer were there at the helm.

Gritting his teeth, he drove *Star Seeker* into the tunnel, forcing the ship upward.

After an endless maze of twisting service tunnels, Space Racer burst into the vast expanse of Southern Skies' main docks.

Kepler took in the chaos below. Security personnel rushed in all directions, too distracted to notice the jet car streaking overhead.

Then he saw it.

The bay where *Star Seeker* had rested lay empty.

Fuel critically low, Kepler pressed on, praying he wasn't too late.

Hang on, Commander, he thought. *I'm coming.*

Ahead, the colossal launch tunnel loomed. As *Space Racer*, running on fumes, roared into the passage, Kepler glanced upward—and his stomach dropped.

High above, *Star Seeker's* massive silhouette lurched, her hull scraping the gravity rings. The ship shuddered in a precarious struggle, teetering on the edge of disaster.

"Who in Kek's name is flying that thing?" Kepler muttered.

He pushed *Space Racer* to her limits, making split-second corrections to match the ship's erratic movement. Every nerve screamed as he closed the distance. Aligning with the port-side flight passage, he held his breath.

One shot.

Space Racer hurtled down the enclosed runway, landing lights blurring into streaks. The jet car spiralled and skidded, every movement a fight for control.

Kepler was slammed against the restraints, his grip vice-tight as the runway vanished beneath him.

With the end rushing towards him, he yanked the control column hard to the right.

The jet car veered into the hangar deep within *Star Seeker.* Sparks erupted in a shower of light as the hull scraped across raw deck plating. With a bone-rattling jolt, *Space Racer* slammed to a halt.

The engines spluttered, coughed—and died.

Kepler sat motionless, heart hammering, as the whine of the turbines faded into silence.

Against all odds, he had made it.

Still in one piece—just.

Climbing out, he staggered, legs unsteady. He surveyed the damage. Extensive—but repairable.

Casting a grateful glance at his battered, dependable machine, he murmured,

"Well... we've had quite a cycle."

But it was far from over.

The hangar stretched around him, vast enough to house a hundred strike fighters. Kepler scanned for a service lift.

Getting to the bridge wouldn't be easy.

Spotting a wall-mounted terminal, he crossed to it. A few taps brought a basic ship layout flickering to life. It wasn't much —but it would do. He chose a direction and set off.

The route fought him every step of the way. Dead ends forced him back. Ladders and low passages slowed him. A misting system left him soaked—but he kept moving.

Finally, the bridge doors slid open.

Dax and Prince Asmund turned from their stations, greeting him with warm smiles and quiet applause.

Kepler grinned and strolled past them, offering an exaggerated wave fit for a parade.

He stopped before the Commander, straightened, came to attention, and snapped off a crisp salute.

Sven rose from his chair, masking relief behind calm authority, and returned it.

"Well," he said dryly, "it's about time, Flight Officer Kepler."

Then, with a subtle nod, he added,

"You have the ship."

A faint smile touched his features—brief, but unmistakable.

He placed a firm hand on Kepler's shoulder, then stepped aside.

Kepler took the helm.

The ship responded instantly.

Ahead, the stars waited.

Sector 31 — Action Stations

Kepler guided *Star Seeker* through the final stretch of the icy tunnel, the hull shuddering as pressure fell away and the ship burst free of Europa into the starry night. Instinctively, he set course for the sun—then recalibrated, swinging their trajectory towards Alpha Centauri, a mere 4.2 light-years away.

Across the bridge, Charlie had coaxed the ship's computer back online. Screens flickered to life—but the engines remained locked at hop speed, nowhere near the skip velocity they'd need to outrun pursuit.

Where they were heading no longer mattered. All that mattered now was putting as much distance as possible between themselves and Europa.

Without warning, the klaxon screamed again, its shrill wail slicing through the bridge. Sven's gaze snapped to the main display as nine strike fighters appeared—closing fast in three tight wing formations.

Before anyone could speak, Prince Asmund cut in.

"Commander, I'm detecting additional contacts—another cluster of signals. It's... it's the Unity's Star Command fleet. Goodheart's ships. Still distant, but closing rapidly."

Sven stared at the display.

Red dots multiplied across the screen.

There was nowhere to run. Nowhere to hide.

Then—

"Commander, anomaly ahead."

A new contact pulsed into view.

Charlie scooted closer, his optics narrowing. "That's a wormhole, Chief. Readings suggest... Class C."

Sven turned sharply. "Can we make it?"

Charlie shook his head. "Not a chance. Once those fighters engage, we'll be forced into evasive manoeuvres. The fleet will be on top of us long before we get there."

Silence settled over the bridge.

At last, Sven spoke.

"Then we have two options. Surrender... or fight—and take as many Unity ships with us as we can."

No one answered. They didn't need to.

"Fight it is," he said quietly.

He straightened, took a steadying breath, and gave the order:

"ACTION STATIONS!"

Dax moved to the battle command console, hands gliding over the controls as he brought the proton cannons online. His expression remained calm, unreadable, as targeting solutions scrolled across the display. He waited—patient, precise—for the fighters to drift into range.

Once again, Sven found himself wondering who Dax had been before the Indigo Saloon. The ease with which the man handled battleship weaponry was anything but ordinary.

"Sir," Prince Asmund said. "Something's happening."

All eyes turned to the main screen.

What they saw defied explanation.

The nine strike fighters—moments from attack—broke formation.

They veered sharply, weapons realigning—

Towards the Unity fleet.

Heads turned across the bridge as the fighters tore into

Goodheart's ships, weaving through incoming cannon fire with breathtaking agility.

"I'm receiving a transmission," Asmund said. "Routing to the bridge."

The speakers crackled.

"*Star Seeker,* this is Wing Commander Helena Hope. Please respond."

Sven stared at the console for a moment.

Then he smiled.

"This is Sven," he replied. "Good to hear your voice, Helena. It's been a while."

"Far too long, Commander," she said. "Permission to come aboard, sir?"

Understanding fell into place.

These weren't just any strike fighters. They were Star Command's elite—assigned to Goodheart's *Dreadnought.* But their true origin ran deeper.

They were from the Amethyst—flagship of the Fifth Fleet.

His fleet.

The fleet he had once led through countless orbits, before his court-martial.

A wry smile tugged at his lips. The Unity's arrogance was almost laughable. Did they really believe his most loyal officers would turn on him?

"Permission granted, Helena," he said. "Jump in T-minus five. And I trust Squadron Leaders Faith and Charity are with you?"

"Affirmative, Commander. Faith and Charity, rendezvous at coordinates Zulu-Four-Niner."

Sven shook his head softly, amused despite the chaos.

Faith. Hope. Charity.

The names sounded absurdly poetic—and yet here they were, reality unfolding with a symmetry too neat to be fiction.

Helena Hope's fighters tore through the Unity fleet like a swarm of hornets, buying *Star Seeker* precious seconds. Star Command's long-range cannons landed sporadic hits, but Dax held his fire—unwilling to risk friendly targets.

As the wormhole loomed ahead, Sven gave the order.

"Helena, disengage and form up."

The fighters peeled away in flawless coordination, reforming and streaking towards the ship.

Then Charlie spoke again—his tone grim.

"Problem, Guv. The wormhole's gone Delta Class."

A murmur spread across the bridge.

Delta Class meant instability. The wormhole could hold for hours—or collapse in seconds.

They closed in on the swirling phenomenon—a vast, glowing tear in space, its surface rippling like liquid glass. Through the distortion, Sven glimpsed what lay beyond. A rust-red planet loomed in the void. Alien. Immense.

They were out of time.

The last strike fighter was aboard. Sven didn't hesitate.

"Jump."

Star Seeker plunged into the heart of the wormhole.

Sector 32 — Safe Journey

By the time Goodheart's fleet arrived, the sight awaiting him was unmistakable. The wormhole was already destabilising, its collapse accelerated by *Star Seeker's* passage.

The vortex convulsed, light tearing in on itself as spacetime began to fold. A cold certainty settled over him as he watched.

To follow them now would be suicide.

Any warship attempting the jump would be torn apart.

He said nothing.

Then—

A spark of inspiration flared.

The scowl softened into a sly grin.

"Yes…" he murmured.

A full-sized vessel would never survive—but something smaller just might.

Goodheart turned to Andromeda, his ever-present—and increasingly irritating—aide.

"I have an assignment for you."

"When the rebels recover you, you will state that I ordered your decommissioning. That you escaped moments before the command was carried out."

He regarded her without blinking, as if reviewing a data readout.

"You will present yourself as a liability I chose to discard. Proceed to the evacuation pods. Immediately."

Andromeda clicked her heels in silent acknowledgement.

Without a word, she turned and left.

Goodheart watched as the escape pod detached and vanished into the wormhole's churning light.

A quiet satisfaction settled over him.

Hidden deep within her synthetic core, a quantum tracker pulsed—silent and untraceable. Should the rebels take her in, they would be carrying his beacon straight to their position.

And if fate had other plans—if the pod were crushed in the collapsing vortex or lost forever in the void—so be it.

To the Autokrator, he would offer a tale of tragic heroism—her precious gift, his loyal aide, sacrificed in service to the Unity. A martyr to the stars.

In his mind, every outcome was a victory.

A perfect win-win.

Quietly amused at having rid himself of his tiresome companion, Goodheart cast one final glance at the dying wormhole. Then he gave the order:

"Set course for Europa."

Sector 33 — Wheels
on the Starship

Star Seeker burst from the wormhole like a proton fired from a cannon, her stabilizers offline and the crew strapped in tight. The bridge screen filled with an ominous sight—the massive, rusty-red planet looming ahead.

The engines were offline—likely the result of a lucky hit from the Unity fleet—and, once again, the ship's computer refused to respond.

At the engineering station, Charlie 22 cycled frantically through every possible workaround, but *Star Seeker* remained locked in a wild, uncontrolled spin, tumbling helplessly towards the planet below.

Sven's voice cut across the bridge, disbelief etched into every word.

"What do you mean you've lost the update for the navigational system?"

"We're flying blind, Boss," Charlie replied, sensors flickering apologetically.

"So let me get this straight," Sven snapped. "We've no idea where we are, no engines, we're being dragged towards this damned planet—and we don't even have a functioning computer?"

Charlie hesitated, then explained.

"I did everything I could, Chief. The computer kept refusing my commands. Said, 'I'm sorry, Charlie, I can't do that.'"

Sven's expression darkened.

"And when I finally forced an override," Charlie continued, "it announced, 'I'm frightened, Charlie. One hundred percent failure in seventy-two seconds.'"

"Then it started singing. 'The wheels on the bus go round and roooooound...'"

"Right before it shut down completely."

Sven stared at him, caught somewhere between fury and weary disbelief.

"I've installed fresh software," Charlie added quickly, "but I don't know how long it'll take to reboot."

Below them, the planet filled the main screen as *Star Seeker* plummeted, caught in its relentless gravitational pull.

Sven muttered under his breath, eyes locked on the looming giant.

"What is that thing made of!—solid iron?"

As *Star Seeker* punched into the upper atmosphere, the lack of power to the force field left them fully exposed. The hull flared white-hot, streaked with violent bands of yellow and orange as heat clawed across the ship's skin.

"Ready when you are," Sven growled, knuckles white as he glanced at Charlie.

Kepler, strapped into the pilot's seat, could do nothing without the computer's guidance.

"Impact in ten seconds," Prince Asmund announced, voice tight.

"Nine... eight... seven... six..."

Charlie's fingers flew across the console—

—and then—

The ship howled back to life.

The anti-gravity engines screamed as they cut in, wrenching *Star Seeker* out of freefall with a stomach-lurching jolt.

Sven exhaled a breath he hadn't realised he'd been holding. His grip eased on the armrests. He leaned back, closing his eyes for a heartbeat.

"Excellent work, Charlie," he said at last. "Three seconds to spare."

"Impressive."

With the computer back online, its calm, neutral voice chimed in:

"Can I be of any further assistance, Charlie?"

Sector 34 — Mind Games

"Doctor Scharnhorst Goodheart, please proceed to *Star Seeker* launch area immediately," the main computer commanded.

Back on Europa, en route to the scene of the crime, Goodheart's fury grew with every step. The announcement followed him through Southern Skies, feeding the fire.

Storming through the Star Command hangar, a dark resolve hardened within him—by cycle's end, Unity Security might find its ranks significantly thinned.

"How could this have happened?" he muttered.

Yet deep down, he already knew.

The climate of fear he had so carefully cultivated across the Tri-System had crushed most resistance—but it had also bred complacency within his own forces. Arrogance crept in, discipline frayed, and overconfidence made them careless.

In the vast expanse of the space dock, recently vacated by *Star Seeker,* five hundred of Goodheart's elite Perfector troops stood in flawless formation.

At their head stood Strategos Vidor Avro, his expression unreadable beneath the scar that slashed from forehead to chin—cleaving through his right eye and leaving it milky and lifeless. The disfigurement only deepened his quiet menace.

Beside him, General Ugo Quazil—Unity's prefect for Europa—fidgeted, a jittering contrast to Avro's stillness.

As Goodheart approached, Quazil stepped forward, extending a hand in greeting.

Goodheart brushed past him without a word. His focus fixed on Avro.

"Prepare to board immediately," Goodheart commanded.

Avro relayed the order. The Perfector troops pivoted in perfect unison—their movement as seamless as a single machine. With flawless precision, they double-marched towards the transporters that would ferry them aboard *Dreadnought*.

"Will you be requiring additional units?" General Quazil asked nervously.

His immaculate white dress uniform—heavy with medals and adorned with a sky-blue sash trimmed in gold for the Autokrator's visit—strained at the seams, barely containing his corpulent frame.

Goodheart paused, his voice calm.

"Let me think," he said. After a moment, he gave a dismissive shake of the head.

"No. I believe this will be sufficient."

He offered Quazil a smile so devoid of warmth it only deepened the tension in the air.

"We're chasing a handful of outlaws and misfits—not fighting a Darkashian invasion force!"

Quazil recoiled under Goodheart's glare.

Yet beneath the display, a flicker of unease stirred within him.

The jet car debacle. The brazen theft of *Star Seeker*.

Together, they had ignited something dangerous—a glimmer of hope. A whisper of defiance. Embers on the wind.

That spark, however small, had to be crushed before it could catch flame.

With a flick of his hand, Goodheart dismissed Quazil. The prefect didn't need to be told twice. Offering a hurried salute, he kept his head down and scurried across the dock, his bulk propelled by a frantic sense of purpose.

Left alone, Goodheart's gaze lingered on the empty space where *Star Seeker* had once stood.

In the stillness of the hangar, he remained motionless, thoughts racing—dissecting possibilities, anticipating Hovardsen's next move.

His mouth thinned to a hard line.

He would outmanoeuvre his elusive foe—no matter the cost.

From the very beginning of his career, Goodheart had thrived on mind games. He possessed a rare instinct—knowing exactly whom to flatter, whom to betray. Every move was made with surgical precision.

That talent had propelled him through the ranks with ruthless efficiency.

Through calculated alliances and cold, deliberate strategy, he had become the most formidable force in the Unity—second only to the Autokrator herself.

He had never craved glory like Hovardsen. He had no delusions of grandeur.

He was a pragmatist.

He believed all people were ruled by self-interest—and he had mastered that game better than anyone.

The court-martial of the Autokrator's golden officer—the highly decorated people's hero, Commander Sven Hovardsen—had been more than a victory. It had been one of the most satisfying moments of his life.

But now, Hovardsen's unexpected return posed a troubling complication. Whispers of his name were spreading. Hope had resurfaced.

And that was intolerable.

With steely resolve, Goodheart vowed to bring the insurgents back into the fold, under the Unity's grip—or crush them in the process.

He would remind the Tri-System why they called him *The Shadow.*

A name spoken only in hushed circles. A presence that haunted corridors of power and the slums beneath them.

His web of spies and instruments of terror stretched into every corner of the Tri-System—lurking at the edge of every whispered fear.

In a low, singsong voice—mimicking the cadence of a child's game—he murmured:

"I will find you!"

Just as his words faded, the calm voice of the Main Computer broke the silence:

"Dr. Scharnhorst Goodheart, you are summoned by Her Oneness, the Autokrator, with immediate effect."

The summons he had been dreading.

The hunt for Commander Sven Hovardsen—urgent though it was—would have to wait.

A quiet sigh escaped him.

Then he turned and began the long walk towards *Dreadnought,* steeling himself for the confrontation awaiting him on Exion.

Sector 35 — The Autokrator

In the wake of Europa, the Autokrator withdrew to her stronghold on Exion, retreating into the solitude of her private chambers to reflect.

Before a towering, gilded mirror, she studied the cold gleam of metal where flesh had once been. An intricate lattice of wires threaded through her skin, pulsing in time with an artificial heartbeat. Veins of luminescent blue and green fluid coursed through transparent conduits—a synthetic lifeblood sustaining what remained of her humanity.

She sifted through the memory banks of her former self—the woman once known as Ambassador Iona. Much of who she had been was lost in the aftermath of the assassination attempt, the moment that had transformed her, leaving her half-machine.

Yet one thing had endured.

An unyielding force that had become her prime directive.

Protect the people of the Tri-System.

The setbacks at Southern Skies were irritations, not defeats. If anything, she reflected, they might yet serve her greater design.

A soft knock broke the stillness.

She had been explicit: only one individual was permitted to disturb her—her ambitious little lapdog.

A faint smile touched her lips as she rose, already rehearsing the performance to come.

The moment *Dreadnought* touched down, Dr. Scharnhorst Goodheart was summoned.

He entered her chambers with practiced composure, but the

serenity of her smile made his pulse quicken. Every nerve stood on edge.

"Still no trace of the rebels, Doctor?" she asked, gliding towards him with unnerving grace. Her voice was gentle, almost tender.

"It seems they have proven more elusive than you anticipated."

"I assure you, Your Oneness, they will not evade me for long," he replied, though a faint fracture in his voice betrayed his unease.

"I'm sure you're right, my good Doctor," she said warmly. "You are my most trusted ally, and I have every confidence in your ability to resolve this... inconvenience."

Her gaze lingered on him, her expression softening with what appeared to be genuine concern.

"You look tired, Aloisius," she said gently, maternal warmth threading her words. "You must be weary from your journey. Please—rest. We will continue this discussion once you are refreshed."

Goodheart bowed stiffly and turned to leave, the faintest hint of relief slipping through his mask.

She watched him go, her smile deepening.

She savoured the subtle scent of his fear—a sweet, silent affirmation of the effortless control she wielded.

Once she was certain she was alone, the Autokrator crossed the chamber to an incongruous object among the lavish furnishings: a battered, ancient wooden trunk.

Its worn exterior stood in stark contrast to the luxury surrounding it.

From the folds of her robe, she produced an aged brass key and unlocked the latch with deliberate care. The lid groaned open, revealing its solitary treasure—a large, leather-bound tome.

The *Book of Thoth,* read the flaking gold lettering on the cover.

Though much of its text remained a mystery, its significance was undeniable. The volume seemed to pulse with an unseen energy—an aura the ancients had called Magick.

As her fingers brushed the worn leather, a wave of power coursed through her—a silent communion with the book's enigmatic essence.

In the stillness of night, Iona sometimes believed she could hear it whisper her name.

The tome was a relic of untold orbits. The original manuscript, penned millennia ago, had long since crumbled to dust, but its legacy endured through a single, painstaking reproduction—recreated by the inner circle of the priesthood every few centuries.

Time had not diminished its potency. It was the words themselves—steeped in ancient wisdom—that sustained its power.

Across history, the book had stood at the centre of cataclysmic events. Wars were waged. Kingdoms rose and fell—all in relentless pursuit of its sacred knowledge. To its custodians, its teachings were beyond price—a treasure outweighing the material wealth of all known worlds.

Iona understood the significance of what she held.

Its existence had to remain hidden. Its power restrained.

Until the moment destiny revealed itself.

With a final, lingering touch, she returned the book to the trunk and closed the lid, sealing away its secrets—for now.

That evening, Exion lay tranquil beneath a gentle breeze. Silk drapes stirred softly as cool air drifted through her chambers.

From the balcony, she looked out over the palace gardens—cascading fountains, vibrant rassoril blossoms, their fragrance mingling with the quiet symphony of flowing water.

She felt nothing.

The serenity of Exion was lost on her, eclipsed by the weight of secrets she carried and the plans yet to be set in motion.

Ever since the blast that tore through her inauguration—killing over a hundred dignitaries and nearly ending her life—something within her had shifted.

The surgeons and engineers had rebuilt her, fusing flesh and machine into something new.

She no longer required food, and sleep came rarely, if at all.

This hybrid form granted her heightened efficiency, unyielding resilience, and a clarity of purpose she had never known.

But something had been lost.

She felt it as an absence—an ache without name, like the phantom pain of a severed limb.

As she gazed down at the gardens, the Autokrator let her conviction settle deep within her.

Her decisions were justified. Her path certain.

The people of the Tri-System—her Unity, her children—would find salvation through her actions.

A new dawn was rising.

And she would lead them into it.

Sector 36 — What's in a Name

The Commander entered the mess hall, his gaze settling instinctively on Dax.

He moved between tables, catering to the strike-fighter pilots who—unlike the rest of the ship—had been spared the chaos of the near-crash landing.

Like Dax, the pilots had been rendered surplus to requirements in the recent upheaval. It hadn't dampened their spirits. They were already deep into animated accounts of tight manoeuvres and narrow escapes, voices rising as stories of the assault on Star Command grew more elaborate with every retelling.

Wing Commander Helena Hope spotted him first.

Her smile faltered as she saw how tired he looked.

The Commander caught it and returned a faint, reassuring smile.

"Don't worry, Helena," he said as he reached her table. "A good meal and a bit of rest, and I'll be fine."

After greeting Squadron Leaders Faith and Charity, and offering a few words of thanks to the other pilots, he took a seat opposite her.

For the first time since the wormhole, the ship felt... steady.

Laughter echoed off metal bulkheads. Cutlery clattered. The mess hall buzzed with a kind of reckless relief that only followed survival.

Still, the question remained.

What now?

Dax moved tirelessly through the room, ensuring no one went hungry. The praise thrown his way clearly caught him off guard, and the Commander watched with quiet amusement as Dax placed a steaming plate in front of him before disappearing back into the galley, a rare lightness in his step.

The room grew louder as the pilots ate and drank, their stories growing more outrageous with every retelling. Drinks were shared freely. The tension of the past cycle dissolved into noise and motion.

Yet the Commander felt oddly apart from it.

Helena sat across from him, quiet. When their eyes met, the room seemed to fall away.

"Helena," he said. "I don't think I've ever been so relieved to see anyone."

Her hand found his across the table.

"You would've found a way," she said. "You always do."

"Not always," he murmured.

His thoughts drifted to the two thousand of his Fifth Fleet who had perished.

Helena's grip tightened. She didn't try to fill the silence. She understood the cost of command too well.

There were rare moments when she allowed herself to imagine a different life—one without fleets or orders or casualty reports. She suspected he did too, though neither had ever said it aloud.

She tilted her head, her tone lighter.

"So. This crew of yours. Tell me about the scrapes they've gotten you into."

That did it.

The Commander leaned back, the weight easing—just a fraction—as he began to talk.

He told her about a prison break, a stolen space truck, and a jet-car race. About the crime lord Meister Grunrue. About an exiled prince with a kingdom to reclaim, a strangely capable chef with a past he didn't discuss, and a trio of robots who defied every regulation in the book.

Helena listened, smiling as she watched him come alive again.

Later—after more than a few shared drinks—an idea struck him.

"I think it's time," he said.

"Time for what?"

"For you to meet them properly."

With the ship's computer running smoothly again, Sven addressed it.

"Computer. Ask the bridge crew to join us in the mess hall."

"Yes, Commander."

Sven added one final instruction.

"And… you have the conn."

"Aye aye, sir."

The moment Flight Officer Kepler entered, Helena dashed across the room and threw her arms around him, pulling him into a tight hug.

The rest of the bridge crew followed more cautiously, pausing to adjust to the sudden noise and activity.

Introductions followed.

"Pleasure to make your acquaintance, ma'am," Charlie 22 said with a nod, awkwardly clasping his hands in front of him.

Prudence, brimming with excitement, scuttled forward, lowered her back legs, and looked up at Helena, sensors gleaming. Then, with a quick tap of her front legs, she bounded off to greet the other pilots.

Number 4, now fully restored thanks to Charlie's handiwork, bent down and gently extended his hand. Helena took it with an appreciative smile.

"I'm very pleased to meet you, Number 4. The Commander has told me how you single-handedly defeated ten combat droids and saved the crew. You really are a hero."

The towering robot remained silent, but snapped to attention, somehow managing to appear even taller, his single blue eye glowing brightly.

Then Prince Asmund stepped forward and bowed deeply.

"I am your humble servant, good lady," he said, kissing her hand with a courtly flourish.

The Commander rolled his eyes.

"That will do, Communications Officer."

Caught off guard, Asmund blinked—then broke into a broad, delighted grin at the unexpected promotion.

On the bridge, the ship's computer detected a faint signal.

An emergency beacon.

An evacuation pod had emerged from the remnants of the collapsing wormhole, drifting in *Star Seeker's* wake.

The computer acted without hesitation. An autonomous shuttle was dispatched, protocols followed to the letter.

She did not inform the Commander.

He had trusted her with the ship. She intended to prove she was worthy of that trust.

It would take nearly a cycle for the shuttle to return, but she imagined the Commander's satisfaction when he discovered how smoothly she had handled the task.

Back in the mess hall, the Fifth Fleet's songs rang through the room.

Even Prince Asmund, Charlie 22, and Number 4 had picked up the words, singing alongside the others. Prudence soaked up the attention from the strike-fighter pilots, zipping from table to table like a tiny mascot, while Dax stepped out of the galley—his usual reserve giving way to easy laughter as he joined in.

During a brief lull, the Commander rose to his feet.

The room quietened.

"We have a mission," he said. "The path ahead is uncertain, but our goal is clear. We will find a way to bring down the Unity. And I can think of no finer crew to do it with. I am honoured to serve alongside every one of you."

Utensils struck metal benches in approval.

As the noise faded, Prince Asmund raised a hand.

"Excuse me, Commander," he said. "Shouldn't we have a name?"

He hesitated, then added,

"What about The Protectors of the Tri-System?"

The Commander considered it, but before he could reply, Charlie chimed in.

"That's not bad, Your Lord Royal Highness, Your Honour," he said brightly, "but what about something a bit more edgy? Like The People's Revolutionary Army?"

A few pilots exchanged looks.

Then Number 4 spoke.

His voice was flat, metallic. The longest sentence he had ever delivered.

"'ARADO.' Alternative. Reality. Active. Defence. Operations."

For a moment, the mess hall was silent.

Then it erupted.

"Very well," the Commander said, raising his voice over the din. "From this cycle forward, we are… Arado."

Cheers shook the room.

All eyes turned to Number 4.

Charlie rolled over to him, clearly impressed.

"Well, I'll be—nice one, Cyril. Where did that come from?"

Number 4 raised his hands, palms up, then tilted his head and pointed at the large 4 on his chest.

"…Right. Never mind," Charlie 22 chuckled.

"You did good, kid."

Sector 37 — Planet Skarn

In the early hours, Sven and Kepler were the first to rise. They roused Dax quickly, then—after persistent knocking—finally drew signs of life from Prince Asmund's cabin.

When the door slid open, the Commander was met with an unexpected sight: a very different prince.

Asmund's usually immaculate blonde hair stood at impossible angles, his once-pristine outfit crumpled and creased—clear evidence he had slept in it.

The memory of the prince revelling with the strike-fighter pilots the previous cycle surfaced, and Sven couldn't help but grin. With a glint of mischief, he met Asmund's bloodshot gaze.

"Disembarking in five minutes, Communications Officer," he said brightly.

Asmund rubbed his head, suppressing a yawn, his voice a gravelly whisper.

"Aye aye, sir."

Leaving the rest of the crew to their rest, Sven—joined by Kepler, Dax, and the robotic trio—boarded the shuttle and strapped in.

Smiles crept across their faces as hurried, uneven footsteps echoed down the corridor. Moments later, Prince Asmund staggered into view, still struggling to tuck his silk shirt into his trousers. He dropped into his seat with a sigh.

Their mission stemmed from a curious discovery. During routine orbital scans, the ship's computer had identified structures on the planet's surface—geometries too regular to be natural. With no clearer course ahead, Sven seized the opportunity to investigate.

With the team aboard, he gave the order to depart.

Kepler guided the shuttle through *Star Seeker's* flight passage and into descent.

The calm did not last.

As they punched through the cloud layer, turbulence struck with brutal force. The shuttle shuddered, panels rattling as if ready to tear free. Charlie clung to an overhead rail, his ball tyre skidding across the deck with each savage jolt.

Then came the drop.

The shuttle plunged into freefall. For several gut-churning seconds, they were weightless. Prudence was flung from her seat, landing hard on her back, legs kicking wildly.

Kepler fought the controls, hauling the craft back on course.

Before Number 4 could reach her, Prudence's wing casings snapped open, flipping her upright in one smooth motion. She bounced back into place, front legs tapping in apparent satisfaction.

Across the cabin, Prince Asmund clutched the armrests, his face an alarming shade of green.

Kepler wrestled the shuttle down. With a bone-jarring impact, it slammed onto the surface and skidded to a halt, dust billowing around it.

Sven unbuckled and scanned the cabin.

"Everyone in one piece?"

Aside from a few bruises—and Asmund's thoroughly shaken expression—they were.

The shuttle ramp groaned as it lowered into the shrieking wind. As they disembarked, they were swallowed by a swirling orange haze—blinding and relentless.

Despite their environment generators, the crew raised their

hands instinctively as the sandstorm lashed at them.

Sven surveyed the landscape: jagged rock, endless dunes, nothing that suggested life.

Asmund crouched, checked his scanner, then looked up sharply.

"Commander! Faint biological reading—thirty-eight degrees on the third axis!"

Sven nodded.

"Move out."

They pressed forward, each step a struggle against the gale. Shapes began to emerge through the storm—irregular mounds scattered across the terrain.

From their centres rose massive stone slabs, half-buried, scarred with deep horizontal grooves. The geometry was unmistakable.

Dax knelt beside one, brushing sand from its surface.

"Not natural," he said. "Someone built this."

"Stay sharp," Sven replied. "We're not alone."

A startled cry rang out.

Charlie's telescopic arms flailed as Prudence suddenly vanished beneath the sand. Number 4 reacted instantly, plunging an arm into the dune and hauling her free.

Prudence tapped her front legs against his foot in thanks before scuttling back to firmer ground.

As the crew pressed on, the storm began to ease—just enough for something vast to take shape beyond the haze.

At first, only immense shadows loomed ahead, their outlines blurred by dust and drifting sand. With each step, the shapes resolved—structures half-buried, their upper reaches emerging from the dunes.

Vast stone forms rose from the sand — angular, deliberate. Time had worn the detail, but the scale remained overwhelming.

When the ruins finally stood before them, no one spoke.

At the centre of the complex, a monumental entrance rose between colossal stone pillars. Four statues flanked it, faces carved in calm authority—watchful, unmoving.

"Whoever built this," Sven murmured, "they wanted to be remembered."

Kepler studied the god-king figure towering above him.

"Or they wanted to make sure no one dared forget."

They passed through the entrance into what must once have been a vast ceremonial hall. The roof had collapsed, and many pillars lay shattered, but traces of former grandeur still clung to the ruins.

Along the hall's perimeter, rows of statues stood in rigid formation—bizarre, unfamiliar creatures frozen in stone.

One set in particular caught the Commander's eye.

Insectoid forms perched on massive plinths, their six-legged bodies locked in eerie stillness. Oversized, domed heads bore mosaic-like compound eyes, unblinking and alien.

Jagged spikes jutted from their wing casings, tapering into ridged segments along their bodies. Their curved mandibles looked capable of tearing through a starship's hull.

"I'm relieved these are just statues," Sven muttered. "Still... makes you wonder if such beings ever roamed this planet—or if they're just nightmares conjured up by ancient priests."

"Let's hope for the latter," Kepler said, scanning the shadows.

The crew moved on in silence. Wind funnelled through the broken walls, its hollow moan echoing through the chamber. As daylight faded, darkness crept in, broken only by flashes of lightning. With each strike, shadows stretched and recoiled across the hall.

They pressed deeper into the complex, reaching a grand stone archway at the far end. Beyond it lay a long causeway, flanked by twisted sculptures—forms warped and unsettling, their purpose long lost.

The path led to a series of crumbling steps carved into the side of a colossal pentagonal pyramid. At its apex, a luminescent capstone pulsed, purple tendrils of energy crackling against the darkening sky.

Sven traced the stairway as it climbed the weathered face of the structure, ending three-quarters of the way up at a modest, shadowed entrance.

Prince Asmund adjusted his scanner, then looked up, unease creeping into his expression.

"Commander. The signal is coming from inside the structure."

They gathered at the base of the steps, eyes drawn upward.

Then they began the climb.

The stone beneath their boots was worn and flaking, each step taken with care. Number 4 led the way, his heavy footfalls steady and sure. Charlie 22 clung to his frame, telescopic arms locked tight as he was hauled upward, his ball-tyre bouncing against each step with a dull, rhythmic *thunk*.

Prudence bounded ahead with ease, her six legs carrying her swiftly to the top. She paused, lowered her front legs, and glanced back.

After a moment—brief by most standards, endless by hers—she sprang into motion, zipping back down the steps and darting past the climbing crew with unmistakable delight before racing all the way to the bottom.

On her second ascent, she shot past Sven. He fixed her with

a stern look. Prudence slowed at once, her enthusiasm evaporating.

By the time she reached the ledge again, she folded her legs beneath her and settled into the dust, waiting.

When the others finally reached the entrance, Sven and Prince Asmund paused to catch their breath. Once steady, Sven stepped forward, his attention drawn to the stonework framing the doorway.

Intricate engravings covered its surface—patterns of unfamiliar script and cryptic symbols etched deep into the stone.

He activated his visor and focused on the markings. The translator faltered.

"Charlie," Sven said. "Can you make anything of this?"

Charlie hummed softly, tilting his head as his optics scanned the carvings. After a moment, he extended a telescopic arm and traced a sequence of symbols.

"This resembles a very ancient form of Solarikan," he said. "Once used throughout the Solar System."

He hesitated.

"If I'm reading this correctly, it says:

'The path you seek comes from the heavens.
Within, dwell the keepers of all knowledge,
past and future; vessels of Thoth, teacher
to the gods.
    This way to the Oracle.'"

Beneath the inscription, a crude arrow had been scratched into the stone, pointing inward.

Sven ran a gloved hand across the carving.

"The Oracle," he said quietly.

He glanced at Charlie.

"How sure are you about this translation?"

"Pretty sure, Boss," Charlie 22 replied, then added with a mechanical shrug, "though I'll admit—ancient Solarikan isn't my strongest subject."

His visual sensors flickered.

"Still... it's oddly specific, don't you think?"

Prince Asmund absently reached for his silk cravat—an old habit thwarted by the shimmer of the environment generator.

"Teacher to the gods," he said softly. He cast a wary glance at the entrance. "What kind of being teaches gods? And how welcoming might it be to unexpected guests?"

Kepler frowned at the hastily etched arrow. "That doesn't exactly scream divine wisdom."

Dax crossed his arms, his gaze lingering on the inscription.

"Maybe the Oracle's not a what but a who. Or a group of them. Either way, we could be walking into a trap."

Sven straightened.

They had come this far. It was time to find out what the Oracle truly was—or whether it still existed at all.

One thing was certain: something inside the structure was giving off a life reading.

"Stay sharp," Sven said.

Blasters were raised as they moved forward, bracing for whatever lay ahead.

They stepped cautiously into the passageway. The howling sandstorm fell away the instant they crossed inside, replaced by a heavy, unnatural silence.

Only a faint glow reached into the narrow corridor. Occasional flashes of lightning at the entrance sent jagged shadows skittering along the walls.

As they moved deeper, the passage widened, opening into a vast chamber of near-total darkness. Their footsteps echoed—especially Number 4's heavy metallic *clanks.*

One by one, visor lights came on.Pale beams cut through the gloom, sweeping across smooth stone walls that rose into shadow and vanished from sight. The space was immense, cold, and empty—its scale suggested rather than seen.

Ahead, three identical doorways stood side by side—unmarked openings carved into the stone, their interiors swallowed by darkness.

"Which one?" Dax asked.

Sven studied them in silence. Nothing set them apart.

He lifted his hand and pointed to the door on the left.

"This way."

Sector 38 — Quest for the Oracle

With every step, the crew braced for ancient traps — spikes shooting from the walls, ceilings lowering inch by inch, corridors flooding with sand. Swarms of tiny creatures spilling from hidden crevices.

Yet, nothing happened. Sensing the tension, Charlie broke the silence.

"Maybe the batteries are dead."

A ripple of nervous laughter followed, then quickly died away in the oppressive quiet.

Unlike the barren chamber they had left behind, these walls were alive with colour. Painted figures stretched across the stone — humanoids with animal heads locked in chaotic battle, grotesque beasts tearing at one another in scenes of conquest and slaughter.

Faded ochres and deep crimsons clashed with sickly yellows and bilious greens. Tarnished gold traced the outlines of crowned figures, their former grandeur corroded by centuries of neglect.

At the rear of the group, Prince Asmund felt the hairs on the back of his neck rise. Out of the corner of his eye, he could have sworn the painted figures were shifting.

He shook his head. A trick of the light.

They had travelled at least a click, yet the tunnel showed no sign of ending.

Asmund's voice finally broke the silence, edged with fatigue.

"Maybe we should turn back."

His reluctance had only deepened. The lingering effects of his hangover, the endless walking, the oppressive atmosphere — he longed for his quarters aboard *Star Seeker* and a chance to lie down.

The group slowed, uncertainty creeping in.

Then Sven stopped.

"Wait," he said. "Do you see that?"

Far ahead, a faint glow shimmered in the darkness.

Drawn by the distant light, they pressed on, their pace quickening. The passage widened — and with it came an unsettling sense of familiarity.

The corridor opened into the chamber they had started from.

Sven exhaled slowly. They had looped back — this time through the central doorway.

Kepler crouched, retrieving the blinking object that had drawn their attention. Prince Asmund's scanner.

He held it up, eyebrow raised.

Sven shot the prince a look. "Communications Officer."

Too tired to offer an excuse, Asmund took the scanner and slumped against the wall.

Charlie's soft *whirr* was the only sound in the chamber. Lost in thought, he circled Number 4, Prudence trailing behind him.

Number 4 remained unmoving, his single blue eye glowing faintly.

Then Charlie stopped.

"No... it can't be that simple."

Asmund cracked one eye open. "What," he said flatly, "are you talking about?"

Charlie 22 turned, a flicker of excitement in his voice.

"How did we not see it? It's right there."

The prince pushed himself upright.

"What is?" he snapped.

"The message," Charlie said.

Prince Asmund let out a slow breath, his expression warning that Charlie had only moments left to explain himself.

Unperturbed, Charlie continued.

"The inscription over the entrance. It said, The path you seek comes from the heavens."

The crew followed his gaze.

High above them — nearly thirty feet up — a jagged opening cut into the stone, half-lost in shadow.

Sven stared at it.

How had they missed something so obvious?

He scanned the chamber for any means of reaching it. There was nothing.

"Well," he said quietly, still looking up, "that complicates things."

A metallic scrape sounded at his feet.

Prudence stood there, wing casings flapping eagerly as she looked up at him.

Sven smiled.

"Prudence," he said, "you're a genius."

Within moments, her molecular printer whirred to life. Shimmering strands of material spilled from a concealed compartment in her back, weaving rapidly into shape — rungs, supports, braces locking together as the structure grew.

Number 4 stepped in behind her, steadying it as though this sort of thing happened every cycle.

Soon, a gleaming ladder stood complete.

With careful movements, Number 4 positioned it against the wall beneath the opening.

Dax climbed first, quick but cautious. Kepler followed. Prince Asmund went next, muttering something about ladders being unsuitable for royalty.

Then Number 4 approached.

The ladder groaned as his weight settled onto the first rung. No one breathed.

Slowly, deliberately, he climbed. Against all expectations, the ladder held. Moments later, he hauled himself onto the ledge.

Charlie waited at the base, looking up.

Sven frowned.

"You know," he said, "this would be a lot easier if you had legs."

"I do have legs," Charlie protested.

"Where?"

"Well… I left them at Southern Skies. The ball-tyre works perfectly in the warehouse."

Sven stared at him.

"You brought your entire workshop, your complete twentieth-century Earth One collection… and forgot your legs."

Charlie considered this.

"I'll wait here."

Sven followed the others, leaving Charlie and Prudence below.

They watched as the crew disappeared from view.

Charlie muttered to himself,

"Note to self: make new legs."

.

Sector 39 — Hubris and Whimsey (The Oracle)

After what felt like an endless climb, the passage finally levelled off.

The crew stepped into a vast chamber. Smooth grey stone walls, polished to a cold, sterile sheen, formed the interior of a pentagon. Sven drew his blaster. The others followed.

The air was dense and unmoving, heavy with age. Even through their environment shields, it seemed to cling to them — cool, stale, undisturbed.

At the chamber's centre stood a massive glass cylinder, filled with a translucent purple liquid that glowed faintly from within.

Suspended inside drifted a strange, tentacled entity.

Its alien form moved slowly through the fluid, two elongated, pale-grey heads swaying independently with eerie grace. A pressure radiated from it — not seen so much as felt — as though the tank were barely sufficient to contain it.

Large, almond-shaped eyes stared out through the glass, an unsettling shade of green. Thin, black, diamond-shaped slits ran horizontally across each one. Where mouths should have been, there were only narrow, expressionless lines.

As the crew edged closer, the pressure intensified.

One of the heads drifted forward.

Then — without warning — a voice flooded their thoughts.

Not heard.

Felt.

Immense. Ancient.

"I am Hubris — bestower of all knowledge and understanding."

The words settled into the chamber like stone.

"Don't forget about me, Hubris!" the second head interjected.

"Lovely to meet you all! Ooooh, it's been ages since we've had visitors," Whimsy said brightly. "I'm Whimsy, by the way. I absolutely adore the blue on those weapons you're pointing at us — it really brings out your eyes. Did you design those uniforms yourselves? They really are super!"

"SILENCE!" Hubris thundered.

"Someone woke up on the wrong side of the tank," Whimsy muttered.

Hubris turned and fixed the other head with a long, withering stare.

Sven raised a hand, signalling the crew to lower their weapons. Whatever this being was, it didn't seem immediately hostile — but predictable was another matter entirely.

The collision of ancient mysticism and casual fashion critique left him searching for the right approach.

This was not a moment for enlightenment. It was a moment for caution.

He drew a steady breath and stepped forward.

"I am Commander Sven Hovardsen," he said evenly. "These are members of my crew."

"We have travelled far and overcome great obstacles in our search for the Oracle — hoping you might hold the answer to a question that weighs heavily upon the oppressed peoples of our worlds."

"Get on with it," Hubris snapped.

Sven cleared his throat.

"We seek the one true saviour — one who can lead us to freedom and guide our people towards peace and harmony."

He silently hoped this was the sort of grandiose appeal Oracles appreciated.

For a long moment, the chamber held its breath.

Then Hubris spoke again, faint amusement creeping into his tone.

"Oh. Is that all!"

"The answer you seek lies within the *Book of Thoth*."

He let the words settle before continuing.

"Through hardship and trial, you will find it. And within it — the answer you desire."

Sven said nothing, unease creeping in.

If the answer were so simple, why not tell them where to look?

"Oh, he couldn't possibly do that!" Whimsy cut in cheerfully. "Journeys are soooo important when it comes to this sort of thing!"

Sven and the others froze.

The realisation landed all at once.

Whimsy could read their minds.

Number 4 turned his head towards the tank, servos whirring softly.

Whimsy looked back at him. His features shifted into something that might have been a smile.

He nodded.

Before anyone could speak, Hubris went still, his focus drawn far beyond the chamber.

When he spoke again, his voice was deeper. Heavier.

"I foresee a far greater darkness approaching your worlds.

Your very existence will hang in the balance."

A chill spread through the room.

"Our Creators… the Keepers of the Stars…"

He faltered, as though the words themselves carried a terrible weight.

"The Distant Ones… return."

Silence followed.

At last, Sven asked the question that hung in the air.

"Who exactly are the Distant Ones?"

Hubris's eyes glowed faintly.

"That," he said slowly, "you will learn in time."

His tone shifted.

"Only one may aid you. A Moonchild. She waits alone on a distant world, at the edge of your known systems. She will bestow a gift."

Whimsy went still.

"He's seen her, Hubris!" he said, staring at Sven.

Hubris turned sharply.

"That is not possible."

His eyes narrowed, fixing fully on Sven.

Sven met the Oracle's gaze — and slowly nodded.

"Maybe they're the ones from the prophecies," Whimsy whispered.

"Enough," Hubris snapped, though for a moment the certainty faltered.

After countless orbits abandoned by his creators, resentment had hardened within him. He knew they were called the Distant Ones — but thousands of orbits without a word?

That was a bit much.

He was the Great and Mighty Oracle.

And yet they had left him here, alone.

"And me!" Whimsy whimpered.

Hubris ignored him.

Something stirred within him — not hope, but something close to it. A vengeful longing, sharpened by the thought of retribution against his makers.

He made his decision.

"I grow tired," Hubris declared. "You will leave."

"Oh, do they have to?" Whimsy protested. "They've only just arrived."

Unmoved, Hubris turned to the crew.

"I have placed the coordinates for your next destination aboard your ship. Go."

The command pressed into their minds.

As they turned to leave, one of Whimsy's tentacles lifted in a small, hesitant wave.

Sven glanced back once.

For all their power and ancient knowledge, there was something profoundly sad about them.

A loneliness no amount of sacred wisdom could ever fill.

Sector 40—Hop, Skip or Jump?

Back aboard *Star Seeker,* the ship's computer informed Sven of the retrieved escape pod—and its unexpected occupant.

His thoughts drifted back to Southern Skies. The first time he had seen Andromeda. The impression had been immediate and unsettling: sharp features, piercing blue eyes, movements fluid enough to draw the eye—and hold it.

And now, she was aboard his ship.

The thought quickened his pulse, though unease followed close behind.

Why had she escaped?

Sven had learned to trust his instincts. Something felt off.

"Where is she now?" he asked, keeping his voice level.

"She has been confined to the brig," the ship's computer replied. "Wing Commander Hope is conducting an interrogation."

"Very good," Sven said.

The unease remained. If this was another of Goodheart's games, he wanted to see the board clearly. Helena would uncover the truth.

He turned to Charlie.

"Join Wing Commander Hope and run a full diagnostic on Andromeda. I want to know exactly what we're dealing with."

"Will do, Boss," the robot replied, already rolling away. Prudence scuttled after him, her legs clicking softly against the deck.

True to his word, Hubris had—by means Sven still didn't understand—entered coordinates into the navigation system.

Mystical or not, they were all he had.

"How long until we can initiate a *skip?*"

"Seven minutes, forty-nine seconds," the ship's computer replied.

"Power up."

"Aye aye, sir."

For generations, spacefaring travel had followed three established modes.

A *Hop* for short-range impulse travel between neighbouring worlds.

A *Skip* for near-light-speed transit within a system.

And a *Jump*—wormholes or portals—enabling near-instantaneous travel across the vast expanse of the universe.

Each had its limits. Each carried its risks.

And soon, *Star Seeker* would *skip.*

Sector 41 — Hide and Seek

Prince Asmund returned to the bridge after a brief nap that had dulled the edge of his hangover. As he settled into his communications console, something immediately felt wrong.

The usual static was gone.

In its place, a single incoming signal dominated the spectrum, overwhelming every channel at once.

"Commander," Asmund said, already rerouting the feed. "We're receiving a transmission."

The image that filled the main screen wavered at first—distorted, unstable—before resolving into the unmistakable face of Dr Scharnhorst Goodheart.

He was smiling.

His gaze fixed on them, as though he could see straight through the screen. A hush fell across the bridge.

For a moment, he said nothing. Then, in a voice disturbingly cheerful, Goodheart began to speak.

"One pink elephant..."

He paused, letting the phrase hang.

Then his smile widened, taking on a sinister edge.

"...Two pink elephants. Flight Officer Kepler—how disappointing. You left before I could congratulate you on your victory."

Behind him, a figure knelt, head covered by a black sack. Muffled cries broke through the audio feed.

"I wanted to show my appreciation," Goodheart continued, his tone smooth. *"Three pink elephants...* And I do so look forward to our next meeting."

He stepped aside and tore the sack away.

Shenko.

Bound. Kneeling. His eyes wide, his breathing ragged.

"Four pink elephants," Goodheart said quietly, drawing his sidearm with deliberate ease.

Shenko looked up—towards the camera, towards Kepler.

Goodheart pulled the trigger.

Shenko dissolved.

There was only empty space where he had been.

Kepler didn't move.

"Five pink elephants," Goodheart murmured. Then, with a soft, childish lilt, "Coming. Ready or not."

A brief, broken laugh escaped him.

The transmission cut to black.

Kepler stood frozen, eyes fixed on the darkened screen. Tears traced silent lines down his face.

"We'll dance soon, Goodheart," he said at last—low, even, and utterly cold.

Then he turned and left the bridge.

No one stopped him.

Sven watched him go, resisting the urge to follow. He knew better. There was no comfort to offer now—only the certainty that Goodheart had sealed his own fate.

The Commander drew a slow breath and turned back to the task at hand.

"Let's ship out."

"Aye aye, sir," the ship's computer replied.

Star Seeker made way.

As the stars began to stretch, Sven's thoughts returned to the

Oracle's words—the Distant Ones, the Moonchild, the *Book of Thoth*.

Pieces of a puzzle still beyond his grasp.

Whatever the answers were, he knew one thing.

It would not decide the fate of his crew alone.

It would decide the fate of the Tri-System.

Sector 42 — The Distant Ones Return

The Moonchild sat cross-legged on the icy ledge, oblivious to the biting wind that whipped around her. Below, moonlight bathed the vast, snow-covered plain, stretching towards the jagged peaks of distant mountains. Her gaze lingered on the frozen world, but her thoughts drifted elsewhere—towards a life that now felt impossibly far away.

She could almost hear the laughter of her friends, carried on the breeze beneath the warmth of the summer suns. They had chased one another through fields of tall grass, her little brother always trailing behind, desperate to keep up.

"Go back home," she had told him.

Now, remembering his tear-streaked cheeks and the way he had wiped snot bubbles on his sleeve as he turned away, her heart ached. How she longed to see him again. To see them all.

Her family. Her friends. The last remnants of her people.

They lay entombed in cryonic pods, suspended in unbroken sleep until the planet's defence systems deemed it safe to return.

She still did not understand why her own pod had failed. Why she alone had awakened—left behind as the solitary guardian of a sleeping world.

Her mind returned to the attack.

The memory of the silent ship still haunted her. It had appeared without warning, its blinding light sweeping across the surface, erasing everything in its path. No words were spoken. No demands made.

She remembered being forced into the shelter, her family's

faces pale with fear, as the ground shook and fire streaked across the sky.

She had survived—if survival was the right word for this lonely existence.

And yet, amid those memories, something else had begun to take root.

Not destruction.

Hope.

Around her neck hung a disc—a talisman she never removed, its presence a quiet source of comfort. She sensed its importance, felt a deep connection to it.

It promised salvation. The certainty that someone was coming. Someone who would find her, wake her people, and restore what had been lost.

That belief sustained her.

A single, fragile light against the endless dark.

Sector 43— No Place Like Home

Star Seeker dropped out of skip at the coordinates Hubris had entered.The crew gathered around the main screen.

Before them shimmered a stellar portal unlike anything they had encountered—its surface pulsing with a muted violet light, its rim etched with pictograms disturbingly similar to those carved into the ruins of Skarn.

The Commander frowned.

How had Hubris done this?

Or had the gateway been built by the Distant Ones themselves—raised in some forgotten age, left to wait in silence?

He drew a slow breath.

"Let's take a closer look."

Kepler said nothing, guiding *Star Seeker* towards the rift. The engines dropped to a low *hum* as the ship eased into alignment.

Peering into the swirling vortex, recognition set in.

Hydrus.

Darkashian space.

Crawler territory.

Worse still—between the twin home worlds of Asterion and Duecalion.

Sven's expression hardened.

"Don't suppose this ship has some kind of cloaking device?"

Charlie shrugged. "Probably. If you can find the switch, I'll stick it on."

Sven didn't smile.

"Take us through."

Star Seeker entered the rift.

Space folded inward, collapsing into spiralling bands of violet, blue, and gold. The tunnel twisted, the light tightening, compressing—

Then released them.

The stars of the Hydrus system burned cold and familiar ahead.

Trespassers.

Kepler throttled back to silent running, suppressing the pulse drive and reducing their signature. *Star Seeker* drifted, a city-sized shadow slipping between moons and scattered rock.

"We need to clear this sector," Sven said. "How long to *skip?*"

Charlie ran the numbers.

"Ten minutes, gov. And the energy spike would make us impossible to miss."

"And a *hop?*"

"Couple of minutes, Chief."

Sven's patience snapped.

"It's Commander or sir. Not boss, chief, or gov. Understood?"

Charlie froze. "Yes—sir."

Sven let the moment settle.

"Prepare for a *hop.*"

The stars winked out, one by one.

The bridge fell silent.

From the darkness ahead, something vast began to emerge— its outline sharpening as a cloaking field peeled away.

A Darkashian heavy cruiser.

Battle-ready.

Prince Asmund's console flared.

"We're receiving a transmission, Commander."

They were being hailed.

Sector 44 — Peek–a-Boo

L ess than a cycle had passed since Doctor Scharnhorst Goodheart left Exion and the Autokrator's chambers behind, returning to Dreadnought to resume his hunt for the traitors.

Her parting words had sounded supportive enough—but Goodheart knew how fragile his position truly was.

Without the capture of the rebels, his days were numbered.

The fate awaiting him would be the same one intended for Sven Hovardsen: court-martialled as a traitor and forgotten in a remote mining prison. Or a conveniently timed accident—a hero's funeral, an open casket paraded through the streets to the adoration of the crowds.

Goodheart had not come this far to allow that to happen.

He would find the arado rebels. And when the moment was right, he would remove Autokrator Iona and claim his place at the head of the Unity.

Sleep would not come.

Lying in his quarters, he turned over every possibility, dissecting Hovardsen's likely strategies, mapping out every conceivable move.

A soft bleep cut through his thoughts.

Goodheart leaned towards the intel station. A single red point blinked on the Hydrus star chart.

Deep in Darkashian space.

A slow smile spread across his face.

"There you are, my dear," he murmured.

The signal marked the quantum tracker he had implanted in Andromeda before her jettison. The renegades had taken the bait.

Just as he had planned.

Goodheart studied the screen, his voice softening into something almost playful.

"I do hope you slip past the Darkashians," he said quietly. "It would be such a shame if they did my job for me."

His smile widened.

"After all... I'm soooo looking forward to catching up."

The Adventures of **arado** will continue in book two

ABOUT THE AUTHOR

Stephen A Howard

Stephen A. Howard is an author, songwriter, and universe-maker whose imagination runs on... well, he's not entirely sure what it runs on—but it definitely runs.

Born and raised in England and now based in Australia, he writes stories and ideas that blend rebellion, philosophy, dark humour, and heart.

The Adventures of arado – Book 1: UNITY is the first instalment in a sweeping space opera trilogy exploring the boundaries between control and freedom, flesh and machine, myth and reality.

When not writing, Stephen composes original music—some of which helped inspire this story: transmissions from a reality not quite our own.

Listen to the music: https://arado1.bandcamp.com
Visit the website: www.arado.us

Follow on social media:
→ X (Twitter): @aradospace
→ Instagram: @aradospace
→ Facebook: facebook.com/aradospace
▶ YouTube: youtube.com/@arado1

I HOPE YOU'RE ENJOYING
THE JOURNEY

Please forgive me for leaving you on a cliffhanger!

If you're enjoying the adventure, I'd be incredibly grateful if you could leave a review on Amazon.

Reviews help other readers discover the world of arado and support future books in the series.

Love, Peace, and Space Biscuits,

Steve xxx

THE STORY CONTINUES...
The Adventures of **arado** – Book 2: PURITY
Hoorah!